The Lutheran

a novel by

Jack Britton Sullivan

Dan River Press
PO Box 298
Thomaston, Maine 04861

§

§

Billy and the Sand

Billy bouncing, face over the edge of the clapboard and eyes into the sand. From the Oregon Territory they'd come in twilight through a shapeless nation and that was in the year eighteen twenty six before speculation created west washing tides and changed the contours of the land forever. Easterly they ventured to prospects more treacherous and unto them things treacherous would be delivered.

So we watch her, jaw and smooth shoulder clattering against the split flooring of the wagon, its wheels so worn that there was talk of eating them just yesterday. We hear the faint moaning of Billy's mothers prayer to the traveler saint Christopher but he's not listening, not here for the land is too vicious, a place where even saints duck in before dark.

"See to the boy," the mother asks.

"See to your prayer mama."

"You tend to him Billy or your father will deal with you."

Billy says nothing in return, her heart as raw as anything about. She shakes her brother of nine with a dirty hand, his tongue lapping at the mounting dust in the corner of his lips. The father's hand reaches through the loose flap to feel his forehead but the boy sleeps on.

"He ain't dead," Billy says.

Since there is no touch for Billy she pulls a latch and falls into the road, the sand becoming white and so begin the Great Salt Flats, those white plains everything about her as she begins to move.

"Cold," she says. "Brother was so cold."

Time passes and with it she walks unafraid to a run, the stars shining like lighted holes in the universe above her, blinking as God himself watches a little girl tread in worn shoes, stepping with a slight pawing of the ground beneath as the wagon pulls away and vanishes in the dark.

By wound clocks it is three thirty three in the morning and the day is the third one of this New Year. Groups of little creatures watch the child run along the path the wagon makes as she tracks it without apprehension. Soon the sun lifts offensively over the mountains and she can see nothing but the bleaching of the white lakes. There's a quick flash before the night sky retreats paranoid to the other side of the world as Billy watches it go.

After a short while she feels another hole in her shoe, a kind of tickling worm there as the wagon turns inland for a securer path. Billy clamors, skips and hops, boarding undetected and they're off again, the absoluteness of no father calling out Billy or a mother check for child. Safe again she cries out for help but it only awakens the brother and brings her trouble so branded Billy shushes as they stop for a dry camp in the open.

"This is bad! Who won't see us out here! Ain't no Christian for four hundred miles at the least and they'll still be looking to kill us! Why don't we just pull up to Satan himself and be done with it!"

"Mind your tongue child! See to Hank. Hank's lungs are scarred from the trip. He was an early baby and a wheezer. Less than a pound upon arrival," replies the father.

"We'd do well to pull closer to the edge," demanded Billy. "Damned fools and idiots stay out in the open in daylight!"

The slap comes from the left and passes to the right. Billy goes down and the mother ignores it completely.

"Thirteen and already a mouth for death and sin!" The father screams, relaxes and begins unloading the wagon before Billy can get to her feet. When she does it shows in her eyes and then hardens. No fear found in those rounded coals ablaze.

2

Dampier Mox saw Billy and her family when they came out of the mountains but they'd given him no look. He'd come four nights from the northwest corner of what would be Nebraska on a bay so ridden into the ground that her nostrils flared with a mixture of snot and blood and her legs buckled with every step. He'd stopped only when she did, leading the animal through the passes, tugging on the reins until they crested the next incline and were off again.

He ran from capture and those trailing had no reason to suspect him other than he was not local and had carried a melancholy expression as he walked through the bar. Dampier was gentle but when he committed the crime he looked like an outcast as he gazed at his reflection while ordering coffee. His mistake had been to cut his eyes in the face of the glass, the flinch enough to bring a half breed drunk to his feet with a piece of mirror made into a shiv. Dampier had disposed of him with fists not meant to liquefy his nose as much as stun him, the Bibles Dampier sold in that monstrous territory left to be swept up by a barkeep who couldn't read a word of it past the numbers. Stopping to save the damned he'd become one.

So now the missionary sits, over five hundred miles from home with six men on fresh horses who have no other deed to serve but the one that takes his life. And there is no salvation except a sleeping wagon he watches for no other word has he spoken or human seen since the incident. But he'll not give them the pleasure of his capture for he's cut from a rougher fabric, spreading the word delivering him from what he does naturally. Dampier Mox knows the trade of killing and has begun his twenty first year with its practice. In the eyes of this mortal sin he only has one alternative.

Dampier looks down the mouth of the makepiece pistol, priming and capping it in preparation, sliding off the animal and sending it to a death it chooses by turning and walking backwards with heaving ribs and bulging eyes. Dampier Mox then pulls back the hammer, hoping to startle the wasteland about and lend a chance to the travelers to bury him. When he presses the weapon against his temple and fires the ensuing click causes him to vomit and his witness to speak.

"I told them not to leave the wagon out in the open and now we got horsekillers without any better sense than to shoot themselves with a gun that won't fire."

Billy stood behind him holding the bay by its mane while smoking a cigarette stolen from her father's stash. She waited for Dampier to turn but he wouldn't, falling to his knees in a shallow marsh where he began to pray, regarding her as a voice he shouldn't acknowledge.

"Stop that! You remind me of my mother who I have to sleep with tonight unless the boy takes sick again and that's likely. Besides, those things don't rise up here. The air is too dense, too frozen to let prayers out. And stop shaking, they haven't followed you. I tracked them back when you came out and if they were going to kill you I'd be looking through your pockets or watching them burn the wagon right now. You got a drink on you?"

Turning he looked with one eye beneath the angle of his hat at the voice, the sun dressing him blue against his slicker. On one knee he rose and turned.

"No, no drink. Who...how old are you?"

"Billy, thirteen. Those are my people in the wagon. Daddy's not good with violence so he doesn't expect it to find him in the open. I got the hell out of there as soon as they fell asleep. We've been traveling nights for safety and then he stops out here for no other reason but stupidity."

"You're foul for a girl."

"You're ignorant to kill yourself when they're more holes to hide in than clouds around this place."

"The sky's cloudless."

"You're still ignorant."

As Billy and Dampier squared to face one another a lone rider came onto the flats behind the wagon and stopped. When he dismounted they didn't see the man or notice him pulling two boiled eggs from his shirt pocket. Kneeling he pinched salt from beneath his boot and with a liberal sprinkling shoved shell and all into his mouth. Chewing he rotated the separated shell and flesh from his gums and spit it onto the ground with a deliberate gnaw for he'd no natural teeth to assist him. Finishing, he pulled two bars of u-shaped iron from his mouth and knocked egg off before returning them to his saddlebag and surveying the land about.

Threadbare the Lutheran had come, Dampier Mox knowing no other figure equaling that outline in the distance. The bounty hunter was Icelandic, Threadbare's home having been the outskirts of Reykjavik where he learned the art of netting fish on their way from the Atlantic to the Norwegian Sea while southwest of him American patriots fell. There he had a family he worshipped and a place where his voice could be heard but so often that won't hold man.

With all in balance the Lutheran awoke one day before dawn and decided he didn't want another moment of this life. He sailed his small vessel across the Denmark Strait and found his fortieth year of life on the shores of Greenland, traversing a sheet of ice with enough density to sink that island before portaging so many more he was forced to pay a toll with his teeth and most of his toes and what man would not emerge scathed and expecting his first dousing of human life from such suffering.

And only weeks would pass before this came in the form of a drunken Inuit from the south rim of Hudson Bay in Canada, a stocky man who wanted to know why white hairs should infect their land and eat their animals like they ate the blacks in that land called America. Having no control of any tongue save Icelandic Threadbare the Lutheran continued to sit humiliated in the man's camp and pay no attention till all were asleep before he acted on that churning hate he felt inside. From this not one of the fifteen villagers would ever dream again for he would not permit them to see another endless day.

With his first taste of killing he walked out of the village and a year later he was on Lake Superior, hired by a voyageur and businessman gone mad, a man with money employing able bodied criminals to carry out tasks too great for the timid. It was simple, if you didn't give up your trapping rights you were removed by the agents and those rights taken. Threadbare excelled at the task and his reputation grew.

For the Lutheran this work was too simple for he soon vanished into the Dakota's and began tracking the guilty on his own, tracing bounties to doorsteps and then back again, that distance dropping Threadbare the Lutheran off quickly into caverns of scathing insanity. In those months of isolation the only voice he heard was his own and that voice was nothing if not pure evil. Those bounties had led him to Dampier Mox and the odds against the missionary were climbing.

Threadbare saw Dampier and Billy a half mile east. Dampier quickly reached out, grabbing Billy's wrist and pulling her into the cover of some low slung Gibraltar bushes, both sliding to land before turning, Dampier placing his hand over her mouth and whispering in her ear.

"He's seen us, lie still. That one's separate from the others following me. He's on his own cause I've heard tales. They must've placed a price on me."

Threadbare the Lutheran ignored them, nudging the front of his gray hat and letting it fall by cord to the middle of his back. A heap of white hair tumbled as he shook, walking over to the wagon while looking back at the two hiding in the distance. Still he wore the heavy breeches and woolen socks of a man accustomed to kneeling on the ribs of boat's bottoms, his wide chest and shoulders clashing with the colorful worm silk about his torso. He pointed at the flap, turning his head to nod as if the pair should be responsible for the contents and what followed.

"I guess your daddy's ready for such," asked Dampier.

"He came this way to settle. Hank's in need of drier weather," she responded.

Without another word Billy snuffed her face from the light as the sun rolled behind a cloud, the Lutheran making his way inside the wagon, the sheet falling on the back cover and then there was silence.

3

The six men chasing him never made it onto the flats. Dampier and Billy found them four miles north, their horses tied together so they sidled and bumped into one another, each man resting like a piece of cut apple around a fire of driftwood. They seemed to be unharmed, sleeping almost, but they were as numb to their surroundings as a desert raindrop.

Dampier stopped long enough to release an animal for Billy from the small remuda they'd left. Her desire to know the fate of her family was stronger than his warnings for she immediately turned and sprinted the animal back to where the wagon sat on the salt flat. He yelled twice but she wasn't listening.

Dampier Mox started to run hoping the Lutheran would follow his tracks and not hers, but she'd chosen to retrace the very trail of his approach and why shouldn't he meet a sure death when saving another soul might be his way to salvation. And is there not in every man's eye and stress that one moment when you see your future in the eyes of a woman you hardly know, a little Billy with soft brown hair and full lips, her burgeoning hips on the cusp of womanhood and how quickly the days would pass before she arrived there. Though tattered he could see in her great sons and daughters. So much so that he weakened as he turned his horse to pursue the young woman with an adoration he little understood.

Billy sat confused astride her horse by the wagon when Dampier broke into the open. Like the men before them the scene seemed too placid to disrupt for there was no harm or burn or cut on the bodies, no thing done to make one think what they found inside was any different from the morning. But Billy had seen.

"They're gone. All of them dead."

Dampier Mox rode up beside her but refused to look through the back flap of the wagon as it flagged in the breeze and returned with a slap.

"Did you..."

"Yes, crawled in there and saw them all. He did whatever he did and then put little Hank between them. It's like he pulled the life out without a scratch, and there ain't none, scratches that is."

Dampier drew his pistol and looked around, riding away from Billy in a wide arc that turned into a circle but there was no sign of the Lutheran, no track of horse or man. Nothing dripped onto that earth or tattooed the ground giving any sign beyond a pack of feeding buzzards two miles north of the wagon. He came back loping and put his hand on her shoulder where she sat in the saddle.

"He's left this place. This is all my fault, I brought him here. He must've hired out as soon as I took off after killing that man. That or he could've been right there when I did it. It was an accident, self defense. Billy, I'm..."

"There's no time for that. We've got holes to dig and people to put in them. I guess this salt won't do unless we get down a ways and I don't know how far that is. Do you?"

"No Billy."

They wrapped each body in tight bundles and decided to leave that place for barely visible rises in the east. Billy drove the wagon and Dampier followed, a week passing before they were deep enough into the Bear River Range and around the Great Salt Lake for the bodies to be buried and marked in a Christian cemetery. They arrived at the little space of pioneers who'd fallen short and they read each of the stones that lay above them and Billy said this would do. While she waited he rode around and looked for a cabin or a sod house in the forest about but there were none, just a rumor that the little burial ground existed and that was true.

Pulling up in the evening and with the stench of her family rising they began to hack graves from the frozen dirt. Several times during the night Billy came out of the hole she dug for Hank, her first task to make them a fire and then a meal and then a place to rest.

Dampier worked until the parents could both be unloaded and placed gently into their respective graves after some twelve hours of digging. He showed no signs of fatigue as he lowered each into the bottom of the rectangular holes, raising his hand without a word to tell Billy he'd do the same for little Hank. She nodded meekly and let him have his way for there was a guilt in his eyes found only on the faces of mothers who send sons out too early, having them never to return as they burrow their way into the bosom of a world that does not want them.

When they'd finished Dampier asked if she'd like to say something and she did, speaking in a raised tone that these are things we should expect when expecting goes unnoticed. He thought this mature for such a young woman so he humbled himself.

"I've brought this to us and there I can never right it again."

Billy's head was down and she was angry, sad, resolving herself to the harshness of living as Dampier delivered his message.

"We lay these before you Creator and ask that you take them as your children to their reward. As I have taken the life of another and am responsible for these lives here I ask that due punishment be given to me and that when they arrive at those gates where you reside might you forgive them for any misgivings and lay them thrice upon me. I ask this in your name, amen and amen."

Dampier looked at Billy, the sweat on her forehead freezing in the falling temperatures. She got to her feet and went inside the wagon, returning with every piece of winter clothing she could find. The coat her father wore she handed to Dampier.

"Thank you Billy."

"Murder is murder mister and you're not part of this. I hope the man that did it pays dearly. And he will. Probably not by the likes of us, but payment is due."

"We all pay Billy."

"You need to get that bounty off your head. I'm a pup but I know that."

Billy picked up a shovel after the warning and began to hollow three shallow trenches where the headstones could rest. It began to snow as she worked, Dampier Mox walking a mile from camp into a ravine for dry wood, the clicking her shovel made hitting root and rock, as obvious to him as the crunch of his very own footsteps as Billy scratched.

Daddy	Mother	Hank
Born in 1790	Born in 1803	Born in 1817
Dead just past a week	Dead with father, by his side	Not ever better
		No chance got

4

"I never had a notion to attach myself to a man but I guess there ain't any choice because the land's too hard for me to do it alone. I don't need another father, the one I buried last month did me fine for the time he was here. If you plan on making me a husband then don't plan on doing it too quick because the winter's thick now and I ain't got an eye on doing anything but staying warm, and if that happens to be in the arms of a man eight years my senior then I guess that can get me to spring. We'll talk then Dampier Mox. Until that time I ain't something you seek to pluck. My daddy's words, not mine."

They had put the wagon on the Big Sandy in the Wyoming Territory and the cold was brutal. The two stopped pushing themselves when they began to see the blazing night fires of men they knew to be savages but saw no person dancing between them as anything harmful. On this night the snow was to their waists in every place they stood outside that ring of heat, each of their four fires built to such a height that the animals huddled between them as did Billy and Dampier, stamping the cold from their feet and adding timber they'd brought from the gravesite as the wind dumped pound after pound of fresh blown cold onto the only other element of survival besides will. They knew others were about, but stopping at the river's edge was their best effort and all must intrude if that be their way.

"I've no need to try anything but whipping this cold. If we wouldn't have copied that bunch of natives with this fire ring we'd be dead by now."

"It works, melted this damn snow to the ice. There should be a patent sold to fools like us out here in February. Still I hope those Indians don't test us. We're not on home ground."

"We're not anywhere Billy. This belongs to Mexico I think, but we ain't with friends."

Huddled together, the seat of the wagon not thirty feet away covered in white powder, each in turn feeding forage to the horses by hand and those beasts closing so near their tongues touched Billy and Dampier's cheeks and the vapor of their breath wet each neck as sawing winds turned horse licks to ice. Not one of the group wanted to take any step that might put them outside the circle. So much so that the tin buckets next to the leathered feet of Billy had to fill themselves and then melt again for the horses to drink steadfast in air so frigid they stood in the very flame of the blaze without burn as the howling increased.

Dampier had to make the last trip to the wagon or else. While he summoned the strength Billy pulled the horses to the ground with such control that before the dawn found them both animal and human alike were resting against one another in a bed of blood warmth. More desperate measures were mentioned but not carried out as Billy grabbed Dampier's hand before he could slash open a mare so weighted with pregnancy that they were willing to crawl inside her and sleep in that womb until all froze or the sun came. Billy stopped him.

"Don't. We need her. She'll have it soon. This things passing, the east is growing yellow."

For another three hours it blew but by mid morning all was still, the wind dying to such a point that the plain was as immoveable as a photograph. When Billy awoke she was eye to eye with the mare and Dampier's head lay across her inside a cocoon of ice and snow. They all rose up at once, manflesh and horse growing from a heap of overblown white.

"The fires are out but the sun's up."

"The cold put us to sleep. That's dangerous Billy."

They got to their feet and looked about. No wagon was visible and the horses could move no further than their most immediate steps without frustration.

The mare's end was wide with birth, fluid falling from the redness at such a drip that it encompassed the only sound on that vast tundra. She was trying to sit back but there wasn't any room so Dampier took the reins of the two closest animals and mounting the larger steed drove them into the snow where they surprised him by maneuvering about as if their very hooves were cloven hot pads immune to the frozen depths.

"Good now Billy?"

"She's going to drop this thing right here."

And open the mother did, with a clot the size of a medicine ball followed by all of the packing of birth and the life therein, its first quarter smoothly, the shape of a mouth, eyes and teeth and then a hang, which Dampier Mox freed by attaching the numbness of his fingertips and running them internally into the mother herself before extracting the foal and bringing it flat against his chest where he unfolded it like a chair while dodging the mothers quivering rump.

"Good Dampier. Let's bring up the fires and let her lick a while if she can get up."

"Let's leave her be. No hurry. What's there to do?"

He helped the little foal around to the front where its mother could see it with fading eyesight. She tried to bring herself up to look out across the plain, ignoring the foal while welding her nervousness to something that approached as black dots on that purely white waste. The other animals had sensed it before her and they were rocking with a seesaw motion in the too deep snow, spinning out spaces for themselves, one bumping into the buried wagon with such force that the animal went to its knees before turning and covering half its body in a snow bank deep enough to keep their wagon sunk to the canvas.

"What do they see Billy?"

"Something's on us. It's working its way through the shallower drifts but I can't make it out."

"Help me sit this mother down the best we can next to the..."

Billy grabbed the mother's head and turned it to the foal before Dampier could finish. Wide eyed and slobbering she began to bleed again and the surface about them soon turned red and before they knew it they were streaked with as much gore as the fresh birth but she would not respond.

"No Billy! Goddammit, lay her out so I can douse these fires. They've brought them to us! Keep her down!"

Dampier leapt from the circle and into the drifts where the four other animals were delirious with fright. He got closest to his own horse and had one foot in the stirrups when the first attack brought a scream from Billy.

"Smell Dampier! They smell the foal!"

Their color yellow in that light, those chilling eyes absorbing the frame of Dampier Mox where he stood half in the saddle, the snow beginning to fall again and the clouds coming to obscure the attack where it started on the upper leg of Dampier as he steadied the horse enough for it to bolt, sitting him directly in the path of a wolf glowing with such thirst for the ecstasy of a red meat kill that he could see its very hate of hunger. Three others had Billy and the foal pinned against a bank of snow, the young horses' eyes rolling with such fear on its entry into the world that it quaked as if existence was dependent on terrible consequence.

"Get off!"

Billy was screaming and kicking while they bit and retreated, the mare struggling to her feet to land one sharp kick to the ribcage of the smallest beast but it did not fold, returning to take a bright red chunk from her front shoulder and she his left ear while Billy's legs entwined themselves like spaghetti, redoubling their fury with a heel shot to the nearest curled jaw of the wolf that wanted her.

Dampier couldn't move but the largest wolf would not attack a second time, pressing him back into the snow and positioning him indecisively, the muscles on the back of the animal's neck swelling at such a rate that when Dampier's head found the wagon he could only fathom that the beast should not be so yellow when there was such mastery of competence in his very eyes, his paws the length of Dampier's foot which dripped his own blood onto the carnivore's forenails.

When he turned his face away expecting the next sound to be bone he was surprised to hear the wolf rip the air with a howl so deafening that Dampier began to cry beneath him, smelling the scent of the predator's vocals, every sense locked on the ghost above him.

"Billy," he said stupidly. "Such a sound this wolf makes."

And what dead man does not calm, quietly looking out of the corner of his eye at the three yellow lobos as they stood in contrast to the snow around Billy and the foal, all howling and moaning before killing from their hind legs.

Stalling for competition the wolves craned their heads, seeing which howl rose up the farthest. And when Billy covered her face the horses gave their necks, the mother falling to the ground exhausted from the attack and the birth and nothing was left for the living except the four explosive shots that came in such rapid succession that muskets must be cooling somewhere on the plain.

The pack dropped in sequence, the wolf atop Dampier getting one in the chest instead of the spine, the rest falling on Billy and the foal, the last to the flank of the mother and all could breathe again.

"Jesus Christ I'm bit," said Dampier. "Who could've made such a shot?"

"Is it bad?" Billy threw off the three animals with effort and freed the foal, the little one finding its mother to never leave again.

"Just tooth marks. I'll not bleed long. Too cold."

Dampier sat with the animal between his legs like a lap dog guessing its weight equal to that of a grown man but not moving without knowing the target would remain still.

"That made the shots Dampier. Get up and look. Six rows north, must've been at least a thousand feet and with the wind in his face. Have you ever seen such?"

"Yes, but it wasn't by the living."

A profile at that distance and little else. Four guns smoking and a figure preparing for another shot. Hands moving up and down barrels while teeth tear packets of ball and powder. Unrifled tubes are packed for discharge while Billy and Dampier sink anxiously into the snow and watch, keeping the animal's heads low, their bodies positioned as breastworks for the killer may seek to shoot again.

But he only goes through the motion and waits, all of the weapons loaded and lain upon the white and deep snow like meat to dry. The fire end of the muskets making four eyes on the plain and he above them pulling a white fur around his shoulders before ducking and hiding himself.

"What does he mean to do Dampier?"

"Let's let it keep for a minute and we'll see. If he means harm after those shots then harm will come. Running will make us dead quicker than staying here."

After a half hour they move around on their bellies amongst the animals and the dead wolves and the afterbirth but all is still. Dampier struggles to push the lobo's corpses over a rise so the horses will settle, but in doing so he draws fire, not from a musket but the shaft of a blue tipped arrow that whistles through the air catching the stomach of his hat where his head would normally be. It burns the top of his scalp as it jumps off, the arrow taking the faded fabric and piggybacking it into a drift fifty feet away.

"I'm not hit! I'm not hit," he screams.

Billy doesn't respond but puts her fingers to her lips, pushing down with her other hand as she wishes her companion to do. Without hesitation Dampier Mox rolls back into the vicinity of the campfires. She can see that some hair has been removed and his scalp is gently bleeding.

"I'm down. Let's stay here. They're all around us," he said.

"That was from the other side. It looked like it come from the snow. I didn't see anybody. It never stops out here. The hardship never stops."

"Makes you want to move to the city doesn't it?"

"Never Dampier."

While hiding in the drifts they hear a dog bark and soon see the animal run between them and the musketman, disappearing gradually with every lope, crawling back up before another step takes it under. They can see the tops of its ears and snout, a whine breaking their gasps, the thing needed to draw their attention away for beside the dog sprang the musketman half the distance nearer his first shot and primed to fire without provocation. This blinded them to their rear and that's when it came.

The screams broke the nothingness behind them as four of the savages rose bald from the edge of the drifts naked to their waists, all hands filled with warring knives above some skin pant not known to the civilized. Their lean bodies were painted bright blue like the tip of the arrow with white streaks angling up from the center groin.

They all landed at once, not making a sound or attacking in haste as if they were equal to the wolf. Yet, in suspending their rage for two heartbeats thump the savages allowed Billy and Dampier to roll fully to their backs, the afterlife awaiting the braves with their first downward slash as a rider on a mount so uniquely powerful that it plowed through the snow killed each of the braves with a headshot that no other man might fit between, the musketman's horse stepping carefully amongst Billy and Dampier where they lay on the ground, not even grazing their loose clothing or mussing the fires. The braves fell like they were being stacked.

The first thing Dampier and Billy saw when they looked up were the testicles of the draft horse. Its rider was covered by sunlight and loading the savages as if they were prey, not allowing them to hit the ground beyond their knees, such an uncommon sight he spoke to explain it.

"I want them warm. All warm. That foal passed with the mother you see. Hitch up your horses past noon and drag the dead away from here if you're staying to be killed. If they cut another dog loose to pull your eyes away you won't see Sunday. Be quick and warned sodbusters. Go due south, along the banks where the snow is eaten by the Green then get off the river when you can."

He turned to look at Dampier and then he turned away again, neither one of them able to see his face or discern what being had brought the destruction.

"You're Mox, Dampier, yes?"

"Yessir I am."

"He's after you, that Lutheran. Threadbare they call him."

"I'm aware of that."

"You goddamn better be! He's much worse than Natrona braves who've been nibbling root. And you're on their land."

Pausing he tied the bottommost brave to the upper one's wrist with a hitch line and shook his head, untying the smallest one and draping him over his lap. Then with four muskets behind the saddle horn and four dead braves about he kicked the massive draft horse and sped off through the deepest of the drifts with the bodies bouncing up and down, their blue smudging the white fur of the musketman. And they all moved on except the dead.

5

The mother and the foal proved difficult to bury. Dampier put leather straps around the mother while Billy carried the foal out and placed it on a bed of snow. They drug the larger animal as far away as the horses could pull, unsure if they could make it through the drifts as the other man had done, knowing there'd be no digging in the firm earth beneath. When Billy went to the river to lift the first stone he stopped her.

"We're not rocking up these bodies. We need to leave here before sundown and that's two hours off. We got to take the quickest route and put some distance between us and the rest of those Natrona's even if it's a foot an hour."

"Say what you mean to say," she replied.

The time it took them to drag the horses onto the fires wouldn't have made any difference for the clouds began to sink low and send snowflakes hissing into the flames. When they were set to leave, Billy having consolidated all of the mounds into one gigantic blaze, the pair was facing a blizzard of lesser proportion but nonetheless belting them with wind and horizontal snow.

"Damn Billy, we've got to get off this plain."

Dampier stood watching the flames dance on the horseflesh with nothing active in his eyes. Billy squatted beside him thinking hopeless thoughts, the scene around them covering all with doom. The rest of the Natrona could come at will, the weather to them nothing more than a change of season, their blood accustomed to the most harsh territory known.

"The water. It's thinner next to the water," Dampier said.

"We got in here and we've got to get out," Billy echoed.

When all was finally settled beside the Big Sandy it was full night. All the supplies they could take from the wagon had to be dug out as well as a path to the river. After everything was gathered each had the reins of a horse, the animal's backs so full of gear they had to be lashed from between and above, the ensuing hump leaving enough room for a rider of Billy's stature but not Dampier.

"What about the other horses?" Billy asked, turning back to look into the darkness. "Never mind. Damn them, they can follow if they want."

The horses crunched the iced edges of the river and broke through with every step, the couple making sure they did not stray from the bank for any distance that would sink them into the frozen mire beyond where they labored. Dampier stumbled, thinking the bank to be sandy and smooth in all places without regarding the balls of solid ice that took his feet mercilessly. But there was no room in the saddle if they were to eat so he pushed forward, his toes frozen and without feeling, the shafts of his ankles stiff with cold as if they did not belong to him.

"You ride a while Dampier. I'll walk."

"No Billy, I'm fine. The Green's ahead of us and then maybe this will clear out down river."

The night wore on and by morning they were within a mile of the Sandy Green merge having covered none of their tracks if the Natrona followed. As Billy looked down at Dampier walking his horse in front of her she could see the cold in his face, the man's lips bluing like the outer shelf of God's water.

"Nothing, just nothing out here," she whispered.

"What?"

Nothing, flat white plains still with a vein of river just strong enough to cut them, talk of a canyon to the south where they could find higher ground but just such talk is fruitless. Likely Dampier thought them more apt to catch fire while

Billy thought of beauty above the earth and things that stir in women which men cannot understand. The man is bone, the woman tissue.

"My mother was good mostly. Crazy Bible she was, to the point she wanted salvation without effort. Yep, crazy Bible she was."

Billy talked to herself as much as Dampier, the older man listening beneath her while pulling them through the cold to some shelter he did not know. For him she handled herself better than those falling on the frontier, going to it and coming back toughened to such a temper she gave off heat through her pitiful rags. Her hair remained full when she removed her coverings and would not grease as if she were static to angels above. Dampier Mox glanced at her as a child but as she sat there on the horse slim eyed and smoking he saw that her shadow was worrisome fond and growing more each day.

"Cigarette Dampier? It'll make those feet warm."

"No thank you Billy." He turned his face down but was caught in the question, aware that she was there and all around him.

The snow stopped and in the afternoon it warmed to above freezing. A rocky ledge projected from a hillside not far from the merging rivers and the two climbed it on broken shale while their horses scattered snow and dug for buried grasses. The rivers made the drifts manageable so they took full advantage by unsaddling their equipment and making a meal of beans and hard bread on the ledge.

If they need make a stand this is where it would be for they'd made less than ten miles and were fearful of another raid, seeing fifteen Shoshone warriors pass in the dim light of evening. An underling of that band approached fearless and yelling up to them in that tongue instructive said there was dry wood and heaps of coarse grasses for their animals if only they would look on the back slope of that very hillock on which they sat. Not speaking a word they huddled together and brought out American currency and displayed leather goods before them but he had no interest.

"Water no! Water no!" He screamed again before leaving, telling them of the existence of a dead mule in the middle of the Green and begging them to take their coffee from the snow and not that putrid pooling sure to bring them harm. As he acted out the other warriors laughed and pointed, wondering how far the young man would go before he made the settlers understand. Finally Billy came to her senses and told the tale to Dampier who was revolving the packing chamber of his pistol for the action to take place when the mocking stopped.

"They don't want us to drink from the river. Something is dead we can't see and they found it."

"We're so out of place here I can't think," he replied.

As the pack turned northeast up the Sandy Billy came to her feet to thank the brave in what she could pick out from his tongue, thinking she was wishing them a farewell. In doing so they saw the effort, returning with a flat palm wave as Billy screamed "no end" in Shoshonean, letting the presence of a painted blue head slip past her fixation where it bobbled on the bright orange hip of the last Shoshone steed to vanish. Then they were gone, their war continuing, making their way against the tracks of the whites and going back from where they'd come, the Natrona not expecting.

6

Billy fell asleep on the ledge with Dampier watching, the evening sun descending in the west as he got to his feet and climbed the top of the hill, to see that the Indians had been right; the opposing side was May and not February for it had been protected from the winter storms. In the clearing an antelope grazed and picked about, erecting its ears as Dampier slid the first piece of shale out of place. Within five minutes, his back against a rock and his face sheltered from the cold he fell into a deep sleep.

As he rested some friend supposed dead and tormented came to him in a dream and began speaking. Dampier Mox remembered him as the slow boy in his hometown, a city he could no longer call home. He recalled him talking of going west scant years after Lewis and Clark had reported to the Congress. And when he finally did he told Dampier the story of what happened in his dream, Dampier being too young to remember anything but his exit and the parting of the people who said he wasn't coming back as he made his way out of town.

The man before him on that slumbering hillock was now in his late fifties and he was well spoken, girded with the furs of survival and survive he did, past the forts of the Army, the last one seen west of Jefferson City as he rose from Kentucky past the final outposts of that time and within reach of wilds he could not imagine. He made his way around some of the early herds and learned to live off the land, having his share of hardships with weather and starvation, going without and making it, brief prayers his only companion.

As he spoke Dampier listened as if awake, feeling himself nod and the cold of the territorial night sink through his wrapping but he could not stir, the man's story pulling him so deep that he reached into the cold touching nothing, the sideways careening of a few rogue snowflakes littering his coat and bared neck.

The man said he avoided the savages when he could, disposing of the rumors by often walking through them with his head down and his horse free to roam, their colors from one coast to the next stretching out in such an array that jealous rainbows disintegrated over their camps after summer rains.

As he crossed the great rifts and rises west of where Dampier lay, the man became tired and wanted to rest but another winter was massaging the fall of that year and the mountains were dressing themselves in early snow. He said he came to a valley at this time but when he looked upon it he couldn't explain its beauty in words for he knew his mind was slow and to flex it might do him harm. So he just sat with his provisions, digging a hovel in the side of a hill, the back end of it lined with rich ore at a depth so shallow he thought grim trolls must've put it there.

Dampier grew tired listening, asking the man in the talk of his sleep to please come to the conclusion for he must return to the woman. "These are not safe parts," he said. Billy heard him.

The man held his hands up, saying that it only took him a month before he was freezing and the first cougar came, sticking its nose into the hovel already knowing what was inside, inspecting the contours of the vagrant to see how best to dispose of him. But the slow boy wouldn't leave for there were mountains to cross and to go forward or return was a sentence of death. So he just sat, day and night for the next seven days, the animal not returning, no marks in the snow to say that he'd come.

With the first gentle cascading of flakes on the eighth morning the cougar burst through the door and attacked the man, pulling him like an infant out into the snow, playing and pawing him because he would not leave. It came back time and again until he was deceased at the bottom of a long drop, broken and dead from his wounds, the cougar ignoring him as food and turning to a herd of sweeter beasts waiting on the plains before him...

The gun went off over Dampier's shoulder and to the right, the report so loud he awoke instantly and began getting to his feet. As he stood he heard Billy sit back in the snow, crunching and digging her bare feet into the ice.

"I've killed," she said. "I've never killed before but I just did."

"Killed what Billy?"

"Down there, those tracks in the moonlight. See where they stop. I stopped them."

"An animal. What?"

"Two legs, big, moving forward up the slope towards you. I hit the thing square. I only did it because we need to get out of here safe. We need to get out of here together."

"What do you see now?"

"I see nothing. It fell in that tall grass but I know I hit it below the neck."

Billy began crying and Dampier pulled her to him, unwrapping himself and rewrapping her, the tips of her toes red with cold and her legs the same.

"Get in close for a minute and then I'll go down..."

Two smashing sounds came from where the Shoshone had spoken along with the screams of two horses. Dampier and Billy froze, their temples thumping in concert. Billy's breath ceased to spiral from her mouth as she pulled into Dampier's neck to find sweat.

"Shhh Billy. They've killed our mounts. Do you have anymore powder for that flintlock?"

"It's in the bag beneath it. It was ready to shoot. I got it ready. I know how to do it."

Dampier got to his feet and went over to pick up the weapon. By the moonlight he could see 1816 embossed on the stock of the musket, CONVERSION BY ERASTUS, VIN FORGE, TENNESSEE branded into the other side. He blew into his hands and motioned Billy over, the pair calming themselves while he primed and assured the fire, the powder clinking down the barrel followed by a ball so carved its very density brought mercy on its catcher.

"You stay here. I'm going around the bottom and see if I can get a shot. You haven't killed enough."

"I need my goddamned shoes Dampier."

"Stand on a rock or get us slaughtered."

Before he left he handed Billy an old French model dragoon pistol turning her wrist over with its weight. She whispered that she could spark it with some accuracy, watching as he checked the spot of her shot and wandered onto the plain, looping around out of sight before she disobeyed him.

When Dampier was gone Billy walked back up the incline and perched above the ledge to survey the situation. She slid into their camp and put on her boots, pushing some rocks forward to steady her aim as Dampier made the corner and approached the dead animals in a light drift of bloody snow. Behind him was an obvious dark red trail gleaming in the moonlight. Billy had opened someone up but they were still afoot. How many was still unknown.

Where the Sandy met the Green the blood trail stopped. Dampier squatted down carelessly, the cut from the arrow on his head burning. He cupped his hands and poured water over his exposed skull, taking a hand full of snow and placing it on the wound. Out of the corner of his eye he could see the legs of the mule, its purple appendages staunch with rigor mortis. The nose of the animal was barely visible in the depths but the smell was overpowering even in the water. Dampier counted six arrows protruding from the beast's ribs, its eyes locked from sight. Fear filled his chest, a new kind more potent than following a blood trail. This fear was on his neck and in his groin, it shuffled in the snow behind him and had crawled over to some rocks after killing his horses.

"They done the same to my mule. It's the blue niggers. The crazy blue niggers."

Dampier turned around and leveled the musket but did not fire. The man on one elbow before him had a hole in his chest that oozed violet froth with every breath, the words he uttered insulting by their very delivery. He had a long black beard and a stark glance accentuated by short crop hair that stood straight and greasy above a head worn from punches and the ties that bind killers. He spat between sentences and had no shame in the attempt on Dampier's life.

"Your bitch has kilt me. I kilt your horses to draw even. Goddamn you for that."

"What were you meaning to do to me?" Dampier asked, then lowered the hammer on the musket and put a hand up for Billy to stay put. She heard the conversation but could not see the men.

"I was gonna kill you and then your missy. There's dimes out for your asses I ain't gonna get cause she's kilt me."

"Why be so honest about it?"

"Do I look like I'm leavin! That goddamned Lutheran's got money strewn like Spaniard's gold all over the territory tryin to get at you two. I don't get a word that comes out of his gobbledy gook mouth but I know five hundred dollars and that's for your hide. Seventy five for the lil' bitch. They sold off the bounty to him exclusively south of the Bighorns. He usually hunts alone. You should be flattered."

Dampier watched him gasp as more and more blood seeped from his chest and he asked to have a look at the girl who shot him. When Billy came around the corner of the stone escarpment Dampier was backing away, the man holding a knife and threatening to get to his feet to do him in.

"That whited out mound of shit Jenkins ain't gonna get this money if I have to kill you half kilt! I've been runnin with him since eighty eight when Virginia come to be a state. We came out of the hills to see Jefferson drink at the tavern. I played him a hand of cards. He said I was rough but rough is what beat the wigs! My beard's been black since then while Jenkins's is dung colored. You know how many years I got on me boy? I've been killin and collectin since before the god-damned survey! I was militia, not Army! We done in Forgott's men at Elberon, ten of us kilt forty in a scout party before the war."

When he could make out Billy he stopped, staring up where the moonlight was shining on her face and reflecting off the snow beneath. His eyes became angry and he lunged, cutting her ankle with a rapid slash.

"Enough!" Dampier was soon on top of him, kicking the blade from his hand and sending it into the icy waters. When he was disarmed he sat back and listened to his own voice.

"I just took a lil' flesh from the missy. You like them young ones don't ya padre? They said you was a padre. No, a missionary. A killer missionary."

"That was an accident. Self defense," replied Dampier.

"Don't answer his questions." Billy was adamant and filling with rage at the assault, her thin leg leaking slow drops of blood into her shoes.

"No matter. You two's gonna die walkin out of here and Jenkins won't collect nothin but bones."

"But he won't know you got to us," Billy said.

"I reckon it'll come through in time that I did the killin indirectly you might say."

"No it won't." She met his eyes, stepping so close she could touch him, her lack of respect for a seasoned murderer too much for the obstinate tracker.

"Why you lil' fair haired wench!"

That was all he got out as Billy raised the dragoon's pistol and fired two feet from his face, sending a ball through his head that thudded to a stop against the stone.

"No it won't," repeated Billy.

Dampier Mox said something before she fired but it came out in the blast, the words making themselves into ghosts and then disappearing. The tracker lay with his head open to the world, all his evil thoughts and proud moments in those Virginia hills and on the western plains up for review and his deeds the same.

Billy showed no remorse. Hardened, damn him in her eyes and thoughts she jumped to straddle the tracker and strip him of everything of value to stead their position. A compass, ten bills, a rodent's hide for frostbitten feet, minor surgical tools and dried meat. She pulled an axe from a pouch on his side and as the man's dead eyes looked up she took the dull side and drew back for a shot that broke his jaw.

"For the horses you bastard!"

"Billy, for Christ's sake girl! He's dead enough!"

She stung him back with a glance three times her age. The look of an experienced barmaid with a shotgun belly and a breast full of hot lead, all that drips from her loins the seed of another and then another and the harshness does not stop there.

"Dampier Mox, you son of a bitch! You better get mean and leave your candy somewhere else! It's hard going because you killed and brought them to us! But I ain't left yet because leaving is dying so you help me strip this man that come to kill us or get your goddamned shirt off and wade out to see what's in that mule's pack! I'm about ten seconds from doing it myself!"

"You need to act your age and let me do the thinking before you go off killing again!"

She spun around and jumped up in the face of Dampier, her breath as hard as any skinners. She was tipped off the edge in her eyes and Dampier was scared.

"Wish me happy birthday Dampier!" She smiled, then stepped back, Dampier with his hand on a small pistol in his coat just in case and in case she knew.

"Wish me happy birthday!"

"Happy birthday."

"Born at dawn, this day, 1812."

Billy saw the look in his eyes as he did the math from her mother's gravestone.

"Okay Billy."

"And no Dampier, I ain't my mama's baby. I can count too. Get that figuring off your face."

7

Billy said her birth mother whitewashed the big trees on their homestead one last time in 1817 but Billy is unsure. From the top the woman used her dead husband's ladder, the mixture of lime, water, whiting and glue more a cosmetic than a preventative for nothing came to kill the giants, nothing at all came to those cool hills of the Oregon Territory.

Then there was the cough, the deep seed of an ailment that would take them both away and leave Billy alone amongst those menacing trees. They let in less light the more frightened she became, a settlement of ten families below her in the valley being of little help as they watched their food wash into the rivers and float downstream during the floods. Their spokesman said they were turning back to an Idaho seventy three years from taking its name and a man named Abijah asked if the girl with the dead parents on the hill had come down but Billy said nothing, by that time having wandered for weeks in the forest after burying her father with her mother and her mother by herself. They had both coughed up the tissue of their lungs and gone forth to do the work they must until the hacking took them and one day they did not stir.

Billy drug her mother out of their sturdy plank house and buried her in the grave beside him, that grave not three months old. She then took all of their possessions and without speaking the language of the tribes in the valley hitched up an old mule stolen from the fleeing settlers and went out to them with a wagon mostly broken wanting to learn how to "go it alone" and they understood. In that camp there were only women and Billy had nothing to fear for all the men were smoking fish and killing bear and they would not return for four months.

One of the elders, a Molalla Tam had taken the white name Sarah and she took a liking to Billy. Sarah was in her eighth decade and said she didn't believe the edge of the earth was filling up with people of other colors but now she knew this was true for Billy stood beside her.

The child was sharp enough to ask where Sarah's name came from if not from the whites and Sarah said that both silent and dangerous gods occupied the face of the world but that didn't mean they existed. Yet the child did not understand, their conversation consisting of drawings and pointing and round eyed stares, Billy taking an axe to show Sarah that houses were made of timber and not only hide but why should Sarah care for her age would pass before the clammy skinned easterners would bring their god and with it their demands.

Billy stayed near the camp, living apart while learning the art of packing dry meat and walking long distances in those four short months. In her lean-to she'd listen to the silence and the structure of their talk but not a word would she take away.

Sarah said she should wait and learn how to handle weapons from some of the older boys but Billy wanted to get back, for if there was anyone to take care of her she would attach herself and go. She knew she was a child and that the world was uneasy and in it alone she would not see a long life, so why not take what she'd learned from the placid Sarah and the cautious women and hold onto it for another time when it would come in handy, which was to be soon.

She left before daybreak on a day when the rains might come. It was mid summer and before she began her walk back up the valley she returned her lean-to to the earth so only scars remained. What came as child left as child but there were skills she'd learned. Ones she turned over in the brain of a human with less than a decade on the earth and in that brain they cemented themselves like a slow genetic code.

It took her three days to get back to the river and when she got there all she found were the old dwellings of the first pioneers. They were burned out hulls, pieces of a past civilization that was not and would never be again. Not in that time and not in that place.

Someone had cooked meat in the houses of those people and Billy wondered if they ever made it across the mountains to that no name Idaho so she looked for skulls and found two. One was a baby and the other an adult, they lay on a floor that hadn't burned but she could not find their bodies and must've been mistaken. Then she walked out back, discovering the mass grave beside the only path in and out of the settlement and all were entombed there, the stench settled out by scavengers and some substance nature had brought to put over them.

Offense and horror had been taken to the group, things Billy could not name to this day. All were joined and disposed of in some manner keeping them whole, not one shot to the head or bullet to the chest, and in doing so she thought of all the things that could've been done but weren't, because we all need reason to explain our violent world.

Not uncomfortable and knowing hardship she took to the task of covering where the invaders had not. And it was sloppy work besides the destruction, not the work of any tribe for they wouldn't make war when abundance gave claim to all land save the spirits. But how were they just put to sleep? The men and women frozen to be thawed, yet there was a pit and the frigid weather did not come there, not for many months if at all.

If one had crazed himself amongst the pilgrims he would've been the last to go and why take himself when the final person had fallen without the least mark? But this couldn't be true because she saw the belt buckle of the large man Abijah where he lay on the bottom, killed first most likely as a resistor would. He'd not done his job and he would not.

Billy's new family found her sixty miles east of the valley afoot and requisitioned from the forest as Sarah had taught her. They approached her in the wagon of their death and saw she was not Indian or foreign and that God himself had planned such a meeting. Billy remembered the father of that band was holding Hank and the mumbling mother was praying, always praying for their safe passage in wilds they did not understand. She burned holes through little Billy when she saw her walking that lane and Billy knew she'd whispered to the father that the child was a demon and if she boarded she'd lead them to damnation. That was the first time she saw him strike, sending the woman back into the pulled cover of the transport and up against the rail to pray once again. And with every movement little Hank coughed, sounding out the same sound that took her natural parents but the sickness did not come for children and would not come for Hank.

The years she was with them they wandered aimlessly like torrential droplets of water on a pitched roof, following rumors of gold and of cattle and of any whimsy the father fancied. His penchant for night traveling and day sleeping maddened Billy for even a child knew that to invite darkness and wear it as a coat was to invite the reapers cut from its cloth. Sleep was stationed in them like a blanket and that blanket was to be pulled tight when the light left. But in '26 on the flats it wouldn't matter.

One day the mother crawled on top of Billy and put her hands to her head to exorcise the demon, realizing Billy knew the end was near. The woman held her and called down the angelic to return her to the depths. And on that day not six months before their deaths Billy would kick her off and never be blessed again, dragging her out and waking the father who turned and said the woman was only worried and the night would be long, so why not sleep Billy, sleep the day away for night is the time to travel.

8

"So that's the way it happened? Where you came from."

"That's it."

Dampier took his hand off the pistol and Billy relaxed. There was sound in the wind and the sound was the river, its waters breaking on the banks where only Billy's voice had been and they could smell a storm. Both looked about at the snow that'd melted and that amount was nil.

Billy's breasts were heavy and peeking through her coat and Dampier was watching them while she calculated the death of the tracker, its ferocity equal to what lay in Dampier's loins, that being all he wanted for the act could be done there as easily as a marital bed. But honor still bound him.

"Cold," she said. "They're cold. Stop looking at me."

Dampier was a solid figure before her, the color of his hair indeterminable beneath his hat, his build that of a laborer in a summer forge, things beneath his coat well hardened and viscous with the lather rich appearance of Billy and the fresh kill. The woman was an ornament for perilous action on that landscape but his fear was slipping away.

"Dampier, we're going to put this guy under ain't we?"

"I hadn't thought about it Billy. You did him, you decide?"

"Days coming. Let's wait for day."

"Your leg there, it's full up with pain. It's got to be hurting."

"It might need a stitch or two but we ain't able to do that right now. It's too cold to bleed long. I decided."

"You decided what?"

"He's not going under. We've done enough burying and he deserves to be eaten. Let's get out of here."

Billy walked back to the camp while Dampier put his hands on his hips and chewed his gums. The dead bounty hunter was directly below him looking up with a broken face into the night but the night was not looking back. Billy called out some question about direction from the bank but he ignored it, staring into the sky with the dead man, its further reaches clear with a disgusting inhuman quality like the sea, as if all souls were absorbed by either or both.

"I'll bury you," he whispered.

Billy saw him act so she brought up the fire and walked out to make water. While she squatted something scurried through the snow making sense of the night. The animal gave her a tack for the clouds were rolling in and darkening everything, the fall of Dampier's shovel taking the ice and minced soil.

"A true chill," she said.

As the last droplets voided her shaking haunches she glanced to the right and saw the prints, staggered to such a degree that the rider must be the weight of three men. Not until she was thoroughly frightened did the Lutheran sit up from his place in the drift, the movement of his body bringing an avalanche of snow that left Billy on her face and covered, her buttocks to the air which he grabbed, standing her skyward before him. Snapping his fingers his equally covered steed came to its feet where it was not.

"You piss on me and my animal."

She couldn't speak or figure the color of his eyes for he looked different at a distance. But he was massive, his gray hat shading her from the moonlight with its abundance of white hair stuffed within. His face was on fire with thoughts of a home he'd never see again and should we not all mourn for the hunter of the killer of men, six from his line having taken their own lives when war could not be found. And Threadbare the Lutheran always sought new war as lesser creatures seek the empty space of peace.

"You man."

"No. Girl."

"No! Your man."

As he spoke he lifted her higher off the ground by the flesh of her buttocks but there was no sex in him. Billy didn't feel the fear of violation as much as pieces of sanity being removed from her condition as her body tilted forward on her own flesh and his fingers, her face slamming into a chest so muffled that there was no heartbeat within.

"The man. Burying the one I killed," she said. Billy kept her face down as he lowered her back into the snow, her chin resting on the side of his hip without anywhere to go.

"You kill." The Lutheran spoke and then reached down to pull a blade from his scabbard the length of Billy's torso. He rammed it into the snow until it struck the frozen ground. He then kneeled down and met her face.

"My God. Jesus God almighty," she said.

The eyes and the breath were competing for an evil so sanctified they'd crossed into the emptiness of imagination. Billy could smell all smells about him and he was the scent of the color silver and red and there is no other explanation.

"Blue," she said.

Face to face, looking into the eyes of the Lutheran as the new day found them. She reached up stoned and bruised with contemplative curiosity like a child.

"Are they blue? Is that color blue," she asked.

The Lutheran caught her hand cold in its reach and consumed it, pulling it into his inner mouth and biting enough so blood let down his lips. Billy passed out as he let her fall into the yellow she'd made, firing one shot in the air and turning his horse across the plains to disappear into a backlog of storm and coming day.

9

When Dampier found her the leg wound was stanched but there was a new opening on her hand. The tip of one finger had been bitten off and it was bleeding profusely into her groin. He covered her and pulled the hand into the pit of his arm while lifting, taking her back to the camp, squeezing with all his might so the bleeding might stop and it did, the ebony bone left to cover itself in time. The bite was a reminder and that was all it was meant to be.

Billy awoke within the hour but would not look at the finger beating in her skull. When she opened her eyes they met Dampier's, the man sitting himself behind a pile of rocks fixed for receiving an attack if that should come. He had every weapon of measure pulled back to cock and was scanning the early morning plains but there was nothing upon them.

"He's done with us for now or you'd be burying me."

"They ain't done with us. Something took the end of your finger off..."

"I put it up to the cage."

"You did what Billy?"

"I put it up to the cage and it was taken."

"What in the hell..."

"Threadbare's come after us. He's about and I stepped too close. He's a man that'll burn the snow."

"He's a son of a bitch that's dead if he comes near."

"Dampier, he's about as likely to come into your range as a tree out here."

They waited but nothing crossed in front of them, each looking at the wounds they'd received since the flats, pieces of their bodies taken by bite or slash or tear. They pretended cruelty was common but neither had been pursued to such a degree they became skittish with every lump in the snow or sound that rang out.

"This finger's got to be dealt with Dampier."

"Dealt with? What do you mean dealt with?"

She didn't say another word until evening and by that time what she thought was superficial had become something else, the bone turning more yellow than white while the skin peeled away like a banana. As the sun was setting she began sweating and the fever came on quick, the storm having fled with the Lutheran.

"Hey," said Billy.

Dampier was walking around nervous and hadn't heard her, switching back and forth between looking over the plains and making a crude rig to carry her southeast to a rumored settlement called Denver. It was days away but the nearest he knew might exist.

"Dampier, can you hear me?"

Billy had her head back and was looking into the rock ledge they perched on. She could see cracks there and in those cracks she thought about creation and her fever and why she need breathe at all. Before her these visions dipped and swung like a skylark dodging clouds of suspended sound. She'd hear the blast of Dampier's musket but say nothing.

"I brought down an antelope Billy. We've meat."

She understood so she asked for a smoke, the man putting one to her lips with bloody hands what seemed like hours later. When she came back fully she saw what had been put before her.

"Eat some of this Billy."

Dampier had gutted and trimmed the animal and it looked like the work of a ten year old. The man had bled it where they slept and had gotten so confused with its innards he'd mostly fried the lungs.

"Pull all that out of here," she said quietly. "Leave it and I'll do it right if you'll keep the critters off. Good shot though."

"Three hundred feet. Decent."

When she tried to move the finger sent her heart soaring, Billy's wind escaping with the spear of pain that shot through her body. She went rigid and tensed, the look on her face a sucking sound only the afflicted know.

"You've got to take care of this Dampier. He must've had venom in him or something."

"That bastard is poison. Why didn't he deal with us? There's nobody out here to stop him."

Dampier knew his options and he'd mastered them before, pulling up his shirt to look at a scar that rained the shapes of worms. He put his finger on it and raised his eyebrows.

"Like this? Shot through and my own fault at that. I was giving one a good cleaning, but it only went through the fat."

"Don't let the rot get in my arm. I don't know why it's moved so damn quick."

"There's no tools. I did this with an iron and ice."

"Make due," she said.

She mumbled an expletive, shifted her black rimmed eyes and pointed at his coat pocket knowing it was there. He put his hands up and she grimaced, changing to a face pleading with Dampier to break the rule. And he did, sliding out a solid English pint of chalky liquid and pulling the cork. Billy disposed of it soundly and then waited.

"I'll sleep and then you do your thing. That was a belt. I'll be down for a while."

"I bought that just before the shooting. The one that got us here."

"I've been looking at it for some time and waiting for you to offer."

She passed out within the half hour but before she did Dampier slid a rock into the fire. It heated black then back to its original color. After some time he spit on it and smelled the sizzle, changing his position to pull Billy's hand across his hip from behind and into his crotch.

Dampier trimmed away all the dead skin, amazed at the advancing infection in such cold. When he'd finished he held it close to the fire to see where the blood still fed, all of the training of working on himself and strangers coming to this barbaric procedure. He spoke to nobody and there was no answer.

"Not enough skin to do it."

Making a ring with his bloody hands he circled the base of Billy's finger and pulled all of the extra flesh towards the top. When he reached into the fire to grab the rock he felt Billy come up and he turned.

"I can't hold it long with just the cloth so I'm going to give it a good press. There's nothing but the rocks to do it with. If we were looking for rocks we'd be in business."

"Mother, say a little prayer," she slurred.

Billy was drunk and didn't understand what she said, squinting southeastward towards the rumor of Denver and then falling back into the ash of her cigarette. She couldn't smell the skin burning but knew she felt pain, her body rising and breaking like whole continents fracturing where she lay, her chips of skin and broken bone traveling in the stomach of the Lutheran as he galloped through a vulnerable world.

10

"There's no use in me dragging you any further. You and the meat and me are making no more than five miles a day going down hill. Can you walk at all?"

"I can try if you'll get us in some thinner snow. It ain't that my legs don't work, there's just no strength down there."

"That's okay Billy. Just stay where you are and I'll get us there. I've made eleven straight and I can do another day. Let me sit a minute."

"Sit as long as you need. The sun's nice, I'll come around. I feel better."

Billy's blood had been poisoned by conditions and the first week she barely awoke and spoke only once. Dampier had taken two lodge poles he found in the snow, ruins of some altar three miles west of where they'd holed up on the Green River. When he came upon the grounds he could see men had been buried there without ceremony, no person lifted to the sky to be closer to their Creator. Dampier surmised they'd been on the run from something and that thing, whether man or beast had taken out several warriors and they lay entombed around him in rocked and deep dug graves. The enemy deserved a burial and had gotten one. Not the ways of the plains and man he thought, and it never would be.

The webbing and wood he needed were lying frozen on the ground as if nature had left them, the group having moved the assorted dead by the same means he'd be carrying Billy, the remainder of his first attempt at a sled lying torn beside her in a heap of broken rawhide. She'd rested on it while giving him directions on the butchering of the antelope.

He'd put it together with the example of the fallen and strapped her to it with everything he had, telling her about the gravesite he'd visited and listening to Billy ask in her delirium if he'd spoken while he was there.

"No, I was alone. It was just the snow, ground and me. But they had everything needed for this rig."

"You weren't alone Dampier. Nobody's alone nowhere."

And that was it, Dampier becoming a horse with a bit in his mouth and Billy strapped to his back, pulling her and as much meat as he could carry across those lands for a week straight in a southeasterly direction until he saw mountains and realized he was more advanced than he thought.

Dampier spent the days listening to Billy talk to herself and in that talk were pictures of oceans and God and small things the short lived ask for. He stopped every evening and made a fire and in his efforts was an unrequited adoration growing quicker than the hillsides brought to peak. The man unwrapped her and cleaned her like a child and emptied her slops and bathed Billy in the cold with melted snow. If a man were sent to find them he would see the marks of the sled three feet wide, a wickiup base without walls being drug across the white, the black pimples of fires and bandages left behind for scavengers to sniff and wonder if they'd be food. And with each cleaning the hand would swell though he kept it clean and humbled his expertise, trying every remedy he knew and all the ones of the wild and those were abundant. He kept the swelling packed in snow for as long as she could stand and he gave her a spicy root named vequellomise he dug up from the ground where mushrooms would be in the spring. As she chewed she smiled, the flakes of the root coming to her lips and the smell of it from the holes of her nose. And he slept little, watching over her on the sled and waiting for the smell of urine or for her to speak, which after eleven days she did, wanting to get to her feet but not eager to see how she stood.

"Let's make an early camp and it'll give you a chance to work that out."

Dampier came around and unstrapped her, lifting up on her arm and making sure she got to her feet. Billy's legs weren't working properly so she just stood leaning until the smell of her body and the drag caught her.

"I stink."

"Your womanly time came while you were going through the sickness but I kept you clean. I didn't do anything disrespectful. I kept you from getting sores. Blood and piss ain't a good mixture in the snow."

"I appreciate it. You're the only fellow I've ever known that would've done such. I'd be violated if I were out here with some ruffian."

"No such thing is going to happen to you Billy. I think we can make this Denver place if we keep going east after we cross the Little Snake. It's still a far piece if it even exists."

But they wouldn't make it, for when they crossed into the land of the Arapaho where borders were as vague as a stream or sand upon stone they saw the fort put like a beggared against the mountains. It was one of the few options they had left.

"We have to go Billy."

"Let's get as close as we can and have a look. I'd rather be killed out here than closed in and murdered by maniacs."

"Let's pull over to those narrows and settle up for the night without a fire and we'll see what comes in and out. I bet it's one of John Quincy's projects for occupying the west."

"That ain't a federal project Dampier. This is Mexico."

Its construction was made of timber half burnt and burning still, the tops of the lashed lumber letting off a strange smoke that hazed the air a dark tan, bringing all eyes to it if you came this way. There was a wide entryway barred permanently by driven stakes, their length no more than three feet and buried to the hilt. The walls of the fort were not manned and there were no guards on duty, every person on horseback passing in and out of its walls busy whipping those outside the perimeter of the fort as they dug through the ice weakened by constant strikes.

And they were a gigantic mix, men of black, brown and white skin all clothed in a different costume befitting the cold of their origin, their picks falling like cut cane. Those not on the ground were tending cattle while they rooted for early grass in the snow. These men were trustees who also had mounts but were left alone to do their bidding as they'd paid the earlier price of the strap.

A woman moved amongst the crew, her walk more a stumble. She carried a bucket of water and from that bucket she'd dip liquid to the men, each one of them rising erect when she passed, taking a drink before handing it to another, some giving her a whack for the coin taken in darker corners the night before.

"A slaver Billy. Looks like they're cutting out the west with a little lesson from the Spanish."

"And going where?"

"They won't stop pushing those boys until they hit water. Criminals mostly, looks like it anyway. A few Indians, probably ones that strayed too far from the hunting grounds. But I swear they've got Puritans thrown in. I see a collar out there digging."

"They've come through quite a few Indians to get here. They'll be a slaughter yet."

"I suppose they just plopped down where they are. Most of the locals are probably still trying to figure out what the hell they're doing making forts from burning logs."

"I don't understand that."

"Signals. Probably got somebody coming in from the east with supplies through those passes."

"It's awfully close to the settlement at Denver if there's still one there."

"It's awfully close to us Billy. Let's go around."

"Not likely," replied the accented voice.

11

Dampier surprised himself by having the gun on the man before he knew there was danger. But the speaker wasn't in the vicinity of his voice, the sound having come from the wind and the wind taking no profile known.

"Come out," said Dampier.

"You're dead if you raise it a New York inch traveler."

There was an explosion from the brush and Dampier's hand was yanked free of the pistol, some fragments of shell embedding themselves, hot lead entering to blister the skin between his thumb and wrist. Billy was turning to see where it came from though she knew they were surrounded.

"Another one padre?"

Dampier's hands went into the air and his chin to his chest, a pellet of sleet hitting his collar followed by another on his shoulder and down the length of his arm.

"Son of a damn bitch! We just had one of these two days back!" The voice was that of an Irishman but there was no face with the words. Then he stepped forward.

"Hello and welcome to Mims Nickel, the only outpost on the face of the earth using vagabond, slave and criminal labor to go nowhere in particular but by all means to get these roustabouts solidly out of the state of Missouri until they each meet their demise or improve their behavior. I'm your keeper and general organizer Mr. Aten Mire Conquin."

The man stepped from behind a boulder three horses across with two trustees to guard him, ragged men riding at an angle absorbing any gunfire to come
from the hunted. Billy could make out only half his face and Dampier none.

"But we ain't..."

"Aren't anywhere close to the Missouri border Mr. Dampier Mox. But your
government is young and deals well with Mexico over these little land ruses.
They'll lease at will to the new states, especially one only five years old and bordering hostile territory. They've a small populace there in Missouri but they've
had all they can hang and shoot and still the misled keep coming through. But
we've curbed that here at Mims Nickel hundreds of miles west. I've taken it upon
myself to be personally responsible after coming from Ireland. Are you familiar
with, no, well, my fortune is made here."

"Save it," said Billy. "You ain't got no reason to keep us."

"Pardon me, but I'm the law until you walk two hundred feet in that direction and from where you stand Billy, well, I'm the keeper. You haven't been convicted in Missouri but you have made a wrong turn."

"He knows Billy," said Dampier.

Before Billy could ask the Irishman dismounted and walked around his two
men, coming over to hold out his hand to Billy, then Dampier, but neither shook
it. He was completely dressed in hides and his hair was long and red, tied back so
tight that blue veins fell from the apex of his forehead and moved to his eyebrows.
Billy could see a word spelled there and that word was MIRE, congenital and in-
tentional and less a defect than a declaration.

"It's MIRE young Billy. Natural you see. Put upon me by birth and the name
by mother," Conquin said.

"Mother of God," replied Dampier.

"Yes, exactly, with enough curved lettering for another but the mother
stopped at MIRE. And you two, usually the bounties will cease to have any effect
west of here but we've had several skirt us and those men have spoken of you and
here you are. And you've done it again haven't you little Billy? Done it and got
yourself in trouble with that finger and that pale beast who sends in letters but
won't come for a visit. But it appears he's visited with you and now I'll collect for
the man and save him a trip, although I'm sure he knows where you are. But you'll
not get out of here. How's the hand, I mean hands travelers?"

Billy began to recede from the center of the conversation. There was fear in
her eyes and her legs were moving involuntarily, sliding over to a rock where the
woman sat down and began to cry.

Dampier could see Conquin was not armed but the trustees were carrying
muskets, each of them having spent so much time at Mims Nickel they were more
zombies than soldiers, their arms something to use on themselves if memories
ever faded to the point of forgetting who they were. And both of these were close,
one a man of sixty who'd robbed a dry goods store out of starvation to help a
brood of grandchildren with dead parents, all of them dying of hunger on a hillside near Shrinks Camp, Missouri three years prior. He paid no attention to Billy
or Dampier, counting the minutes while looking at the stirrups of the other trustee
who was more menacing but offset with a head much larger than his body and

eyes that bugged out at Dampier and Billy. He was an enlisted man dropped off at Mims Nickel when he cut the throat of a quartermaster who'd been drinking and making light of his ailment, the top heavy man having caught cholera from the conditions of butchering and the alkaline creeks where everyman drank. He was gaunt and crazed, having taken the infection and lasted it, that sickness being strong enough to water his bowels but not mean enough to kill him.

Dampier moved back and forth underneath his hat brim till he got the eyes of each man, the first one empty of caring for he'd seen so much hardship that any alternative was feasible. But the man stripped from cholera was not ready to give and there was no making sense of his glare, he looking at Dampier and then at the back of the Irishman's head who was watching Billy and taking steps towards her.

When Dampier drew into his coat with his opposing hand he felt the big pistol catch, giving him time to look into the eyes of the old man once more. Dampier didn't comprehend the look for it was pleading and merciful, a summons to take him off the face of the earth and he did, the pistol bucking backwards in his hand, sending the old man to sit with those children never fed from his crime in the beyond.

"Better off," said Dampier.

The Irishman was just reacting to the situation when the trustee with the enormous head opened fire on Dampier but missed, the ball from the musket whizzing over his shoulder and lifting up a mound of sleet behind him, those pellets falling so heavily they absorbed the impact and the ball sat smoking.

"Sorry," said Dampier.

Once more with these strange apologetic utterances Dampier sent a shot from a concealed popgun into the face of the man who came off his horse as if jerked by a rope and then there was silence, only broken when the Irishman had taken in the assault and given it the full treatment of respect.

"Will you be killing the horses also," he asked.

"No, you'll do," replied Dampier. "Step away from the girl."

"You're in no position to give orders. You've killed two perfectly good slaves and it'll take two years to replace them."

The Irishman named Conquin moved quickly and when he did Dampier took three paces back to prime the big pistol, his swiftness like a dueler, tearing and jamming at such a rate that if the man marked with MIRE would've ran Dampier would've seen every step and he would've died anyway.

"Stop," he said to Conquin.

But Conquin came, quickening his pace to win the sprint, lowering his body to ram Dampier but he fell short by a step, the weight of the man caught by the hand of Dampier Mox, a deflection and enough of an avoidance to stop the killing.

"Enough," said Conquin.

The MIRE on his forehead was standing out as if it might burst. He fell over himself in the sleet and raised back up, snapping his fingers in the air, the ensuing folly of shot so tremendous that both Billy and Dampier went to their stomachs and put their faces in the ice.

But Conquin stood, hoping they'd understood the game by looking behind them where fifteen mounted trustees sat training their sights on either bounty that moved. Eight had fired and were reloading.

"You wouldn't have gotten out anyway," he said. "They're straining not to kill one another and you two would be prizes. Now stay down and let's see if we can't do this without any more problems. And oh yes, did I say welcome?"

"You did," replied Dampier. "Why don't they turn those muskets on you? It'd make for a shorter sentence."

"There's worse out there besides me. They feel safe here. Most of them that is."

12

Sleet rained for two days and neither Dampier or Billy had any idea when day or night came. They could hear voices outside the door but that door ended a tunnel, the remainder winding to the outside. Both had been blindfolded when they entered after being released from the backs of the animals packing them in, their confusion growing with every step.

Now what held them was a jail of earth and ice. In the corner there was a hole deep enough for waste with a wooden top over it, the same wood that made up the door, a timber structure solid enough that when someone passed it sounded like they were speaking from the stomach of a human.

Dampier awoke in the pitch dark thinking it was their first day but he was wrong. He crawled around on his hands and knees, finding the cold wall leading to a permafrost ceiling before finding Billy. She was whimpering and balled up in the corner, kicking at him when she felt his touch with words about sleep and permanent nights, about what you do when there is no light and no light there was. He said he would marry her and take her away but before them now were people wanting to bring their end.

"We'll make boys Billy. And a girl. Now wake up and help me."

"Get me out of here or they'll be nothing left Dampier."

"He'll die for what he's done," he replied.

Dampier left her and continued to search with his hands for food or water but there was none, only a wooden ladle left in the dirt and with that ladle he began to take out the wall, digging and scratching at the tomb holding them until he could smell alcohol and meat, the wall breaking in front of him and the light of a late evening flooding in. He reached through and his hand felt something warm. It was a large bowl of stew and beside it was a liquid with a camphor smell. As he began to bring in the food a voice spoke.

"Take the water first. That's seventy two hours without a drink. I'm glad you found the spoon and figured it out. He thinks it's funny to place the ladle and see if they can get to the outside. Lucky for you they've been leaving the door open so these walls are a little thin from the heat."

Dampier put his lips against the hole and then an eye. The woman had her hands on her knees and was speaking while looking over her shoulder at a trapper with the face of a monkey. He had her skirts up and was pushing against her and in those last few words he finished.

"It's the best living I can make and they want it all hours."

"Are you the woman from the outside?"

"Yeh, that's my other job."

There were other words exchanged but the woman didn't respond, walking out of the tunnel to receive an order before coming back. While she was gone Dampier brought in some water and gave Billy a drink, which she took before huddling down in the corner again. He sipped it slowly when it was his turn, coming back to meet her eye in the hole, now widened with a persistent kick to the size of a coconut.

"Put that hand of yours through and let me have a look. Then give me her finger. That mean bastard is about somewhere because they got folks out looking for him to clear the bounty. But they ain't no use in you dying before justice is served."

"We ain't bad people," said Dampier.

"I ain't referring to you."

Dampier put his hand through and could feel her pulling out pieces of shrapnel and laying in some clean stitches. He wanted to scream and pull back but she'd done something that kept him from feeling pain. Wiggling his fingers he knew it was just the cold.

While she was working another prisoner came. Instead of looking through Dampier let his head hang and left his arm on the outside. The act itself was over with so quick that as he fell asleep he felt a tug and she was done with his hand.

"Give her a bite to eat and then let me have her paw."

"Why can't you just come in here and do it."

"Because Clarabelle doesn't want a ball put in her brain and the last time she done something stupid she was in Frankfort underneath a Tulip Poplar with her sister's husband and now she's here."

"I thought this bunch was from Missouri."

"My sister is from Missouri and that's all it took. Now I got to service the worst."

Dampier did as he was asked and Billy ate mightily, asking no questions about their position or the opportunity to escape. When she was done she went back to her corner.

"Billy, she'll take care of that finger if you put it through the hole."

Billy didn't move as Dampier stood in the dim light giving him some sense of her expression. Everything warm in that cave was running over his back and around his neck but that illumination was also fading for she'd given up. Then Clarabelle joined in, her head coming through the opening, dirt falling to the barrier of a solid block of ice as she spoke.

"Billy! Get up from that goddamned corner and quit your sulking! There's worse fates I'd trade for besides yours and you ain't got no need to die because you can't keep a wound clean! Give me the hand!"

Billy obediently came to her feet with the abrasive treatment. As her hand went through the hole Dampier could see the mud on her face streaked with tears and he knew the episode with Conquin had done her in. Billy needed for the hardship to stop but it doesn't on command. Even though he had peddled the word of God he knew some things happened without reason.

"Listen, Conquin says that animal is coming two days from Sunday. There's talk he's going to split the pot with Threadbare, the big Lutheran, you two know him?"

"That's his name."

Clarabelle was on her knees speaking to Billy and Dampier at the same time, the girl having come around knowing there were other women surviving in such an environment. Clarabelle had served enough of her days at Mims Nickel and was prepared to go if Billy and Dampier would join her.

"I know about the money and I won't lie to you, five hundred and seventy five in coin is a ton but once we get out of here it won't do me no good because if we get stopped we're dead."

"How're we going to get out of here? We're blocked up in this cave and you ain't got no leverage to get us outside."

"Billy, shut your mouth and stop acting your age. I'm Miss Clarabelle and Miss Clarabelle's got the sweetest cakes there is."

"She ain't worth nothing Dampier! She don't know nothing about nothing!"

Billy broke, leaving the light to go to her corner. Dampier was convinced Clarabelle was their only chance so he continued to sit and listen. He put his head as far into the hole as he could to see what he was dealing with. What he saw was a woman of middle age with dark eyes and hair fading towards gray. She wore what she'd been convicted in, a long skirt of green covering wide hips muscled from the drudgery of the acts performed on the prisoners seeking her company. There was a hardened beauty in her appearance and a certain finesse in the tilts of her head as she explained what had captured them on the plains.

"Listen you. I've got to go up and deal with Conquin so I need to wash myself and make a show. If I can get a couple in him, which he'll have already had, I'll try to soften him on the exchange with that Lutheran."

"Thank you Clarabelle."

"You're welcome. Ya'll sit tight and I'll be back."

Clarabelle was surprised that full night found her in the courtyard of the fort. Prisoners were milling about and several asked for her favors but she told them she was going to see Conquin. As she walked the winding stairway she saw some of the trustees beginning to play the barbaric game of rabbit and gun, the one Conquin loved to watch from his quarters high above the prisoners.

He was already doing it as she ascended, giving signals to the trustees as to which way the man should run, an Indian brave of seventeen who'd stolen one horse from the remuda at Mims Nickel and had received a year's punishment. A sentence much better than hanging for Conquin knew the trustees were offering him a break onto the plain with the promise of freedom if he made it through their first shot.

As another Indian explained the situation to the boy in Shoshonean Clarabelle turned back to the well to wash herself, leery of the folly being made of the boy's life.

"Dern that Conquin. Dern his goddamned Irish hide," she said.

The Ute was let out the front gate and told no matter what he did only one shot would be fired. His eyes were big and his body lean, anxious to run into the darkness with such speed that no ball could find him when he reached a vaporous velocity, the pure essence of his freedom enough stealth to remove weaponry from the equation. But as much as he sought that false security Conquin sought a grievance against it, completely confident that the Belgium smoothbore, still six years ahead of its time could take the prey at any speed and in any condition. So he lifted it from its case, beaming and half drunk, walking out onto the perch for just such an occasion. As he wiped oil from the barrel and stock he thought he smelled snow, but those days were passing.

Bursting, Conquin saw the boy sprint out and then turn, the rumors of the savage's dexterity firm in his mind. There was so much moonlight he gave the benefit to the boy; twenty, thirty, then forty yards before he even put down the tumbler of spirits in his hand and picked up the gigantic musket he'd sat down to light a smoke. He thought he might urinate for the sake of vanity but saw the Ute near the rocks where he'd picked up Billy and Dampier.

"Whoa, he's out there. Time leaves me."

Conquin lifted the weapon to his shoulder, flipped up a primitive sighting pin and touched off the trigger. There was an explosion, the boy given a lead of four feet and he ran right into it, the back of his shoulder being torn from his body. When he fell there was a flurry of activity from some of the trustees but Conquin calmed them instantly.

"No! No! Not yet! One shot! Let's see if he gets up! Hold on now!"

"What awful entertainment for these brigands and scoundrels. It's a shame I have to do such to keep them in chains," he added.

There was a lull and then he saw the Ute get to his feet and begin stumbling back to the fort. His arm was completely torn off and he was walking the wrong way, having no intentions of tempting another shot or inviting the fort to break its promise.

"He's coming back! Okay then, go ahead! No shooting!"

As soon as Conquin got the words out of his mouth a pack of the most violent trustees bolted and began closing on the boy. When he saw them he turned and in the shock of lost blood went for the rocks and cover. He was holding what was left of the torn side of his body, beginning to chant in low pitched sounds for resolve to quicken in his dying blood.

And just as the lead trustee, a man in the skin of goats and boars had sewn the gap to a mere three gallops he made the last mistake of his life, one committed while Clarabelle knocked on Conquin's door, the man forcing her to wait for the Irishman saw the trustee violating the one rule of the game by pulling his pistol to shoot through the boy. When he did it only took Conquin a second with the pace of eight arms to touch off another shot from the smoothbore, a blast so accurate it took the head of the trustee and the chest of the Ute.

The rest of the men stopped their horses and wheeled around to look up at the parapet in the distance where Conquin was screaming as if they'd killed his very instinct with stupidity.

"One shot! Always one shot! We've never done it any other way! The other, an act of God!"

As a pack the trustees turned their mounts and made their way back to the fort. Amongst them there was talk of the consequences of infidelity to such a man as Conquin and in that talk a few spoke of drawing their pistols but not one did. One man, a Jew by the name of Ira said he would no longer carry the weight of his guns when they went to goad the quarry. He said it made him feel awkward and that was enough for Conquin to seethe.

"Two dead and such a big man you are, shooting from the window in the dark."

Conquin spun around to see Clarabelle standing in the middle of the room. The musket was still smoking and there was oil all over his hands and the MIRE on his forehead was light, almost imperceptible.

"Never talk first and don't ever enter uninvited," he said.

"Then find something else to pickle brute."

"So Clara, how..."

"Clarabelle. My mother gave me all the letters so use them."

"So Clarabelle, how many have you had today?"

"Six trades, but I spent time with the prisoners like I was asked."

"And they're a rough sort aren't they? That little woman is the devil incarnate."

"She's not yet fifteen and held up in this place. I think I'd turn out mean myself."

"You think she might have an interest in plying your trade if she's given proper incentive?"

"If you want that Mox character to come back in your dreams and kill you."

"Oh, he's the next to run, hang, or shoot. I'm suffering from overcrowding and it looks like that slow fellow he shot has cut the cholera loose in the fort. I think I'll cull the ones who have water in their stool and run them onto the plains. That way the rest of us won't suffer. In Europe we learn from plagues. Here they're easily taken care of by space."

"Who'll be left to defend us?"

"Oh yes, the delightful savages and tribesmen. Well, we'll be able to keep enough I suppose. Besides, we're right in the middle of their buffalo track. If they haven't come by now, well."

"Why don't you get that bounty man..."

Aten Mire Conquin spun around from his leisurely stroll across the room to face her. He stopped her from saying another word with his eyes, his teeth bared as if he'd bitten the side of his mouth.

"Clarabelle, we'll deal with Threadbare as little as possible. In fact, if I weren't sure that by letting them go he'd spend the next twenty years toying with them then I would commit myself to a first release, not being Missourians and all."

"He ain't a money person?"

"I think that bastard would rather copulate with his horse than collect. He's a strange type they say. Although we've not had time to converse, I do know he has several stories behind him that are disturbing to mention."

"Even for a devil like you?"

"I'm refined Clarabelle. My games are the games of lesser men at times but I wasn't raised on the potato or its liquor. I've been trained to do what I do by the best."

"Killin."

"Incarceration and control. Now come over here and lie down."

Conquin made his way over to a four post bed and took off his shirt. The skin on his back was a series of black and blue marks, the edges of each red and swollen. Clarabelle saw the marks and sat down at a writing table.

"What's that from?"

"A lady in your profession. A miner's wife from the Sangre De Cristo's to the south. A big lady, wasn't happy with the price of the act so I, ah, relieved her of worry. But she struck quick."

"You killed a whore?"

"Scare you?"

"I've seen worse than you and took their pocketbooks."

"I've seen harder than you and ate their livers," he retorted.

"What do you know about that Lutheran?"

"Mere tales."

"Any I'd be interested in hearing?"

"Do you wish nightmares for yourself and others?"

"Anything to dull the pain of Mims Nickel."

"Hot coffee?"

"No."

"I wouldn't share it anyway."

13

Conquin said Threadbare the Lutheran operated by choice in the republic but there were no borders when it came to his lust for the chase. During the months Iturbide ruled in Mexico he'd wheeled off the pursuit of a Frenchman who'd been killing randomly and at will in the northern section of an infant Louisiana.

The man he turned on was one of meager offense, a looter, a robber of the wealthy and their crops, but one who continued to frustrate former militia by making wild dashes into the lands of Mexico where he spoke the language and blended in affectionately amongst the people of the uppermost river. He would settle in for a month at a time and as the educated read Europe's books of revolt his fame grew out of proportion to his crimes and he became a waiting martyr from Mexico City to the reaches of an unknown Texas still twenty plus years in the making.

When Threadbare first smelled him the martyr had been in modern day Baton Rouge hiding his wife and child before riding into New Orleans. The man was overrun with gold, searching for waterfront land from plantation owners, ready to invest an enormous sum he'd lifted from a Spanish dignitary in a brothel in that tempestuous city.

And the Lutheran had the knowledge, but he didn't follow the martyr along that tree lined road leading to the edge of the sea. Nor would he go ahead of him to wait, paying the small sum it took to turn the holders of the real estate or to kill them outright if they refused him his bounty. Instead he watched the wife and child as they made their way from seclusion into the shops of escaped Mexicans in the streets of Baton Rouge, speaking their tongue, bringing attention to themselves as the kin of the great liberator.

The Lutheran listened to their talk, making use of the shade of the Spanish moss hanging plentiful in the afternoon light before taking them, ripping each in turn from those singing streets in a melee so rapid that as he passed not one stepped aside or made their way to avoid his trek. The people of Baton Rouge could do nothing.

"It's just another story of killing Conquin."

Conquin was pulling Clarabelle down onto his chest and groin but she wouldn't allow him the pleasure of ending his storytelling, asking for the details of an earlier Louisiana and Mexico, of what the killers had done and why the Lutheran turned from the Frenchman to chase an apple stealer into southern deserts and over rocky hillocks infested with death.

"He didn't chase anybody anywhere Clarabelle. He took."

When Conquin made the point she came off him and grimaced. He slapped her so hard she fell into the floor.

"I'll end these things where I end them Clarabelle! You're not done with me till I say so!"

Clarabelle got to her feet and started to draw the small knife she kept in her bosom. Yet she knew what was coming in the days ahead so she demurred and asked again.

"He took you said. Took what?"

"He took the wife and child on a six hundred mile ride north of Baton Rouge and left them in the central plains east of here. He let the land do the punishing. They walked for days and still there was nothing. No word of where they'd gone for the husband. No rumor or speculation for the law. He answered to nobody and nobody asked. The bounty was cleared and the husband was finished. Lost his martyrdom, lost his mind."

"So the women still thrive?"

"Have you ventured east from Mims Nickel?"

"Yes."

"Alone, through the Borger Flats? And before that, there's mountains, grasslands, everything possible in a horizon."

"No."

"The genteel don't thrive and pride is buried quick out there. I'm candy amongst those tribes. Candy without crunch. They aren't a settled bunch. They've already had it with folks passing through their grounds and the year eighteen thirty is still four years off. Now leave."

"To hell with you Aten Conquin."

He turned a finger to his brow and said "Aten Mire Conquin whore."

14

Conquin got the group together at dawn the next day and lined them up in front of the fort. Among the twelve were men who suffered the sickness and those wishing to try their luck in any direction. In still a smaller unaffected pack was a veteran of the revolt against Britain. Aged and experienced, he knew the men dying of cholera could be helped if he could just get them free of the enclosure.

Before he left the veteran told Conquin that if he'd clean the musty chambers and boil through the water the spread could be checked. "Fewer would die," he said. "I don't give a token for you Conquin, but less of these men would perish. I've learned the lessons of war and this thing taking men to bones can be slowed."

"Then Paterson, stay with us and counsel me on such," replied Conquin.

Conquin was cheery that all would die on the plains, allowing the veteran a pardon because he couldn't remember his infraction.

"Conquin, you're a bastard deserving hell but if you're willing to let the savages and the mountains have a go at me instead of rotting here then I'll leave with the lepers."

"But remember there's no bond set on your life. You've always been free at Mims Nickel. Regularly free to leave at will," Conquin responded.

"I was born to a mother carried off by me and I saw Delaware become the first state. I'm not a speaker but what lies before me is easier than what I've done thus far." Paterson was looking up at Conquin in the cold, his words laced with such heat that the Irishman's horse took a step back and tried to turn but Conquin scolded him.

The twelve men being evicted from the fort were half dead except for the old man, an enormous black who'd killed his owner and a vaquero who spoke no English but had been smart enough to separate himself from every man known to be vomiting or lying in his own waste. Mumbling in Spanish he spoke of a woman in a scarlet robe wearing a black mask and she was the one who brought the illness but he wasn't content just avoiding her.

"*Lo visto. Es una bruja. Lo visto,*" he said.

He and the black tied plague masks around their faces, pitiful filters cut from their own winter coats. Conquin laughed at the two, then had Clarabelle stitch a primitive cover of his own.

The twelve looked out at a stretch of clear range to the east. An imprint of jagged mountains could be reached by crossing a snow swept mass of geographical mazes, land pocked by drop holes and hunters who knew no men besides themselves and in knowing would think nothing of manflesh for their racks. But the disciple named Paterson calmed them, saying that people of God, though sparse and circumspect on that plain would still be pleased to help fellow travelers such as themselves.

"But you won't find them men, not in the shape three quarters of you hold. Your very legs will break with the pestilence you carry and I hope since you've likely brought it here that the deaths are hard. Manson, forward these slugs out with your quirt and send them on their way. There's enough light now," Conquin said.

The trustee named Manson, a small dark headed man with a heavy beard and tattoos of leeches on his neck hit the first man he could reach and in doing so sent the sad column onto the plains, riding around them as a group, sparing no man a lick.

"Hey big black nigger! Come closer and let me have a chunk of that back," he said.

"I'm free of you Manson. Stop that horse and get off. You can have all this nigger you require."

Manson wouldn't respond, popping a couple of the men with frames like scarecrows as Paterson moved to help. Manson drew his pistol and considered shooting the black but knew Conquin would be moving for sport. And he was, for during the whole episode the Irishman was rushing up to his chambers to grab the smoothbore, returning to the gate on foot to murder a Mississippian named Vill between two standing men, his body so wasted he was being dragged by the black and the vaquero, his wrists cracking and snapping with every step.

"Close shot," said the black. "But good he done that. Man's a goddamned mess."

The vaquero said "*Vill de Mississippi*" and then watched him die.

Much later Paterson got them to a stream with a sidebar hot spring and while the black rocked it off the vaquero explained what followed them in the tracks he saw. His plumage of words were misunderstood and frustrating, each of the debilitated men guessing what he meant as he waved his arms and moved his neck about in animal motion.

"Indians," Paterson said. "He says the mud steps are from lighter ponies."

"Those Paints won't draw close with this bunch. They've likely seen us crossing though we ain't eight miles from the fort. We look too damned wasted to give a fight. No worries now." The black said his peace, crossed the stream in the cold and returned to the work he'd started as the short day ended and the sick men sat pensive on their demise. Just as he lifted the next boulder the vaquero crossed behind him, pulling down his plague mask and grabbing the black by the shoulder.

"No! No Indios! No hay Indios!"

He was talking to the black but looking back at the huddled men as they sat at the feet of Paterson awaiting his command, each in need of wash and food and warmth, none of them able to give another step, their stomachs drawn tight with eyes hollowed in their skulls. The black pulled away from the vaquero and pushed him into the cold water, warning his death in a language not understood though the gesture was obvious.

"Alright then Mexico!" The black's tone was answered with the drawing of a knife by the vaquero and a lunge ripping the sleeve of the black's coat.

A man named Raxley Hide who was wracked with the effects of cholera saw the coming death of the vaquero and intervened, picking up two black stones the size of oranges and dispatching them with such accuracy that the knuckle of the vaquero and the knee of the black were already swelling before they could surmise the origin of the assault. He then fell back and waited for them to find his eyes on the opposite bank. When they did he tugged on the pants leg of Paterson, nodding with a deliberateness given to a court's judgment.

"The Mexican sees the track of the Lutheran. Now listen you two, the lot of us is dead, though I do appreciate you helpin with what we got Mr. Paterson. So they's eleven of us left, Vill got his, so that leaves eight bodies in the next two days and I can tell you many more's comin in that fort or I wasn't born in Georgia. So if you and the Mexican kill each other that leaves Paterson and he's too old to flee bounty."

He picked up his chest with weak lungs and prepared to finish his statement, a median strip of his own waste making its way down his leg and dissolving in the snow. There was a cough from one of the men and he turned to it before looking back at the vaquero.

"Now you there cowboy, you get what I'm sayin, so step back over the water or the next two stones will slay two giants."

The vaquero did as he was told, throwing the knife into the snow and wading back to sit next to Raxley Hide, both he and the black lifting their plague masks in unison. The rest of the men had come alive and were listening to Hide as he gave last rights and worth to their plights, commanding the black and the vaquero to do what they must to bypass the quelled brutality.

"He's gonna come kill us for fun but not till eight are dead. He ain't the type to waste shot so I suggest you two stop killin amongst yourselves and ease the rest of us a little. I'd like to try and eat somethin though I know it ain't gonna keep in my gut. Also, one of us needs to give Vill a decent burial. The man was a Christian and he'd want a proper headstone. Have we got a gun amongst us?"

Paterson produced an enormous cap and ball sidearm stored in his lower back. "We're fixed, though my powder's low."

"Good then," said Hide.

He tried to continue as the others mumbled between themselves. One asked for water, everyone agreeing that sustenance was necessary except for a man named Leekes. He lay face up and was staring at the sky, a beaver slapping its tail on the water to his right, composing himself to build a dam as the black had done.

"Now we're seven sick," said Paterson.

"That count's apt to come down Mr. Paterson. Ya'll do what you can," said Hide.

The black and the vaquero would go with the pistol to attend to Vill two miles west in the dark. Paterson told each man slowly that if he heard a shot and it wasn't to defend themselves he'd nurse the sick until his rage overtook him and then hunt them down.

"If that Lutheran comes and the healthy ones are dead we're all dead," he said.

Paterson then loaded the gun, handing it to the black who traded it to the vaquero for his knife and the two laughed, the black gesturing so the vaquero understood that if the devil wanted them it wouldn't matter. But the vaquero already knew, crossing himself and the chest of the black who raised his hands and said "bless you."

They left instantly and were gone for an eternity, the blackness extending out to the lithosphere where no shot would be heard, the voices of the vaquero and the black falling silent once Vill was buried. No one would ever see them again.

15

Paterson carried each man across the stream, unrolling their beds so they could rest while their feet dangled in the spring and the vapor warmed them. The scalding waters were quarantined from the cold so much so that Paterson had to breach several sections for the task at hand as the putrid water swirled, its smell the scent of sulfur and with that sulfur cholera and his own contagion. He stripped the seven and bathed each like a child, going to them with bread and the freshest water he could find as each settled just being in his presence.

"Don't be ashamed men. Wrap yourself in your blankets and let me wash these rags. Stay close to the edge and the cold won't get you. Our brother has done a tremendous job with these rocks."

A late winter's snow arrived while he tended the men throughout the night but not one knew of its arrival, each of them summoning enough strength to slide down into the warmth of the spring when the tip of a toe or a once fleshy back felt chill. Paterson the grandfather and the servant of man took each of them into his rough arms like sons, their illness striking to such a degree they were half his size.

In the morning two more were gone, their skin tucked to every curve of their bodies with faces frozen in smiles. Paterson couldn't control his emotion and stood before them stunned.

"You done good for them two Paterson. Silens and Scripts. Missouri and Missouri. Both mankillers and reprobates like myself. But you showed meanness ain't the best way. They was happy to die with your help. They gave out pleased," said Hide.

Raxley Hide had been the only one to improve physically during the night, the others having succumbed to the conditions of Mims Nickel and although they carried their end they'd been given dignity for a brief breath of time.

Paterson looked around at the five remaining, Hide being the only one that could speak and sit up. The others refused to dress themselves though their crude clothing was rock hot dry and waiting. Their bodies were prunelike and stunk from their excretions. Paterson had made sure they were kept clean, but he was losing the war.

"I can't do anymore," said Paterson.

"You done plenty sir," replied Hide. "They're blinkin and happy to know it ain't so bad now. They're talkin with their eyes."

Paterson came up out of the water and made his way into the cold barefooted and shirtless. He was overcome with the sting of the ice and his body smoked and he could do no more save prayer. Behind him the five were spread out like disassembled parts, limbs overlapping as each body starved for moisture and Hide took it upon himself to take over, pouring water down thirsty men's throats and he too became the deliverer, shortened in span and time but still a protector as Paterson walked away seeking moments from the condition of himself. He'd defended others and gone to the point of destruction, both Hide and Paterson mixing with futility while sacrificing for men they barely knew. We should thank them as they reel on that empty landscape like a mirage.

"Paterson! Paterson!"

The old man had strayed dangerously far from camp and Raxley Hide was scared.

"Paterson! Can you hear me!"

On his second call Paterson returned, his entire frame numb with shaky steps. He took the waters himself and faced Hide who'd been alone for some time.

"Sorry to leave you," said Paterson.

"No matter, they're all gone. And the other two ain't likely to return."

"It's just us then."

"Looks like it. Any thoughts?"

"Not a one."

"I know somethin."

"What do you know Hide?"

"We're goin to have company."

16

Conquin let them out after he killed Vill. Dampier and Billy wheeled in the daylight, their eyes looking about as if seeing earth for the first time, a place with high wooden walls where men were being eaten away by their own incapacity to clean themselves, each day one more falling sick and then another. The rumor was that Conquin now refused to go amongst the prisoners or the trustees after he had his fun that morning. He was sitting in his shooting perch high atop the fort wall sighting on something but would not fire.

The men of the fort were busying themselves with various tasks. A third of them were sweeping dirty snow and cracked soil while the others were boiling linens and butchering cattle so close to one another that as the crisp white sheets came out to dry they were hit with slashes of blood then sunk back in.

These boilers and butchers were eyeing one another and when the trustee in charge turned his back a maniac from the butchering lot reached across the fence of his pen and stabbed a washing attendant in the neck as Billy watched. Several loads of clean and wet linen were covered with the geyser spew from his neck and yet another shot rang out from Conquin's steeple, its reverberation caught by the fort's walls.

Dampier grabbed Billy's hand and ran behind some empty wine casks, ducking and peering over the lids, seeing no man sidestep or look to see who'd been hit for the infraction had already been penalized. A smaller trustee had dismounted and was rolling the body of the maniac out of the butchering pen and tying his legs together with a lariat attached to his saddlehorn, pulling the limp frame as he bounced over the floor of the fort and out the front gate. The trustee carried him several hundred yards and released the man next to a pile of corpses before returning.

They both got to their feet and looked up at the perch where Conquin had shot and he saw them, gesturing that the ball had gone straight through the neck and wasn't that ironic that he should pick such a spot. He then lifted his finger and said "one moment," moving like a mime in the confines of his surroundings, ducking in his room and then back out in a drunken stumble to put his hands in the air and dig like a rodent, knowing he'd allowed them escape and that all decisions were his in that fortified world.

"He wants us out here to see it all," said Dampier.

Dampier had continued to chip away at several of the holes he'd made since Clarabelle left. He sent Billy through one to remove the lock from the door, the key hanging conveniently with no guard posted. It was Conquin's way of testing the mettle of his prisoners and how quickly they'd give up after the rumors of Mims Nickel's solitude was upon them and they were placed in the very cave of their worst nightmares, when all they had to do was find a tunnel and exit to an alternate confinement.

"Clarabelle could've helped with that information and we wouldn't have stayed in there till now," Billy remarked.

She was disgusted and filthy but her spirits were creeping upward again. Billy was showing signs of determination and Dampier was hoping she wouldn't get them killed.

"That's a cruel damn joke," he said. "I was wondering why everybody moved about so freely. But they ain't no freedom. You're invited to cage yourself if you want."

"These men don't look to be in that good of shape," said Billy.

"They got it bad here. Let's find Clarabelle. I guess we've got some chore to do or something."

"Up here! I'm listening, waiting for the shooting to die down. He's pretty drunk. We can expect another one," screamed Clarabelle. Sunlight was filtering through her hair as her body bent to throw a basket of Conquin's clothes over a line to dry. She was on a scaffold, a thing with arms reaching upward to join at a perfect sunny angle for the keeper's clothes.

"It was the gallows but there really ain't no use for it with such an accurate pop as that smoothbore has. Come up," she said.

Billy and Dampier made their way over several assorted crates to the northwest side of the fort until they saw a hidden ladder. When they stepped onto the platform Clarabelle slung a pair of stockings through a noose and pulled Billy close.

"The wilds won't get that mean old bastard Paterson. I expect he's still alive out there somewhere. He won't leave them boys to die if he can help it. I got to know him during his time."

Clarabelle was acting as if she were talking to herself, using Billy and Damp-ier to fill up space on the scaffold so her words stuck to something.

"No, you ain't saw it come to being. But it has."

"What?" Billy and Dampier insisted she tell them but she finished her task before speaking, yanking them into a tight circle.

"Some of the sick were cut loose and Conquin was so drunk he sent this wily woodsman named Paterson out too. A couple of others that were healthy went also. Them plains ain't getting Paterson. No they won't."

"That ain't got the least bit to do with us," said Billy.

"The hell it don't! You see the death cart they're filling up over there. I'd had a notion for the three of us to escape in that thing but I'm not too sure we wouldn't be dead by nightfall if we did."

"We need to go out one at a time if we do that."

"You don't want what's killing this fort Dampier. And if you slide around with them bones you'll get it. Paterson warned me but Conquin won't listen. Besides, if we're going we need to slip past that damn Lutheran because he's ex-pected to be about. But I can tell you he ain't likely to come in these walls with the number that's going out."

She broke from them and stepped away indecisively, her plan foiled by na-ture in a form more devastating than weather. The Lutheran or cholera, the latter less traumatic.

"You two think it over and let me know. My plan ain't going to work and we need another. But I can't lie to you, once we're out somebody has got to split up and find old Paterson. If we go traipsing around in threes we're done for. And if we fool with direction or take some animal trail we might as well shoot each other."

"But Clarabelle!" Billy called after her, softening herself with a convincing tone to query whether any questions had been asked about their bounty, but the woman was gone.

They both watched as she went up to three of the roughest looking trustees and spoke to them in turn. Each one smiled as she approached and gave her a look when she left. The last one was Manson to which Clarabelle gave the longest parcel of time, looking up at the man as he supervised the dividing of the washers and butchers from his horse. Dampier was already skeptical about the change in her behavior whereas Billy was completely convinced.

"Billy, we might make our own way on this one."

"I guess we can get out of here when we're ready. I'm pretty ready now," she said.

"What's next?"

"Next Dampier is a bet."

"Give me the odds."

"The bet is that Clarabelle goes straight up to Conquin's roost and lays into him with every goddamn stinking word we said."

And she did, hesitating long enough to pick up three chops from an Asian cutter. When she got them to his room he threw the meat over the edge of the fort and pulled her inside. Before he shut the door he looked out at Dampier and Billy who were sitting on the scaffold biding their time while looking out at the fort, their eyes dodging for holes and breaks, lapses in judgment, wondering what words were being said.

But they shouldn't have remained sitting so high in the gallows for their bodies were like neon markers on the sea. Obvious to those inside the fort and to the one watching them from a small hillock to the north through a spyglass, his hands kneading the scalp of the large black while he counted the toes of the vaquero ten more times.

Within the last hour he'd drawn close to the man Paterson that Clarabelle praised, watching him as he tended the ghost Raxley, a man who'd survive his cholera and remain robust once the skin of a few antelope were put on his bones. But there were no bounties for those two, whereas the vaquero and the black's had fallen into a cistern of paperwork in their home states only to be resurrected by the Lutheran's influence and reputation. He could revive lost bounties under mountains of paperwork as well as he could kill. There were others in Mims Nickel set up in a similar fashion and if the Lutheran didn't do his homework he did little else.

While boxing up the toes of the vaquero and the scalp of the black in separate containers he periodically looked to Billy and Dampier who were arguing with Manson, a man particularly suited to be exploited by the Lutheran if he wandered too far past the death pile. He'd been one of the first queries the Lutheran sent, and the only one where a governor personally wrote him to take the man's head if he could.

When the Lutheran heard the hooves hitting the stone pathway he came to his feet and began scratching addresses on the individual parcels with a coal pencil. At the last moment he decided to route them together so he ripped open the cloth around the black's scalp and put it in with the vaquero's toes, retying and marking the package JEFF CITY, MISSOURI-CENTRAL ROUND just as the horseman made the hill above him. When the right people got the package the pay would be nice. And if it weren't held for him someone would lose his life.

The Lutheran backed out of sight amongst the boulders and when the express rider came within his grasp he leapt. The boy was knocked off his horse, the sacks of mail for the prison flying in all directions as the rider crashed down and began bleeding from his mouth.

The Lutheran put his gun on him while he went through the mail for Conquin, stealing updates on new arrivals and requisitions for various supplies from the nearest outposts. When he finished pilfering he put his parcel in a greasy black saddlebag and on the bottom he placed a coin for the boy he'd hit. He then drug him over next to the only tree with standing limbs and tied his horse to his leg, walking backwards to drag out his tracks while watching over his shoulder.

When the carrier awoke he thought himself stupid for not looking for the tree. He looked for Indians and bandits and animals but he never thought he'd be unsaddled by a scrub oak grown large. Shaking his head he got up and looked at his horse.

As he stepped into the saddle he leaned backwards just missing the Lutheran's blade. The bounty hunter was considering a more viable form of butchery and needed to practice. But the boy was let go with the Lutheran's human cargo aboard, the package to be delivered within the month if he was fortunate.

The rider bolted by the gate of the fort and threw the mail against the doorway. When it hit there were curses as it exploded and four trustees descended to separate its contents. The last they saw of the rider he was running south, his arm against his bleeding lips hoping the disease wasting the place wouldn't follow him to his next stop on a distant lake, every step defying the presence of the Mexican authorities he evaded.

17

Conquin had them tie a rope to the mail and he pulled it up. He'd been waiting on word from the Lutheran but the man wasn't coming. The bounty hunter was perusing the prison from his post as the day wore on, seeing that the fort would kill itself if he'd just wait. He was bold enough to build a fire but the tower guardians of the fort were too sick to care. They looked out at the smoke but it wasn't unordinary in their condition.

The Lutheran ate nothing that night and watched no more, riding his horse out to see if the man Paterson and Raxley Hide had left the hot springs. They had so he followed their tracks southeastward knowing that Paterson would go for the nearest settlement. The track said the man Hide had a weak leg and it looked like Paterson carried him at times, the furrows in the soil and snow becoming heavy and deep, the man so light that Paterson could've been toting a sack of meal or a bale of parched feed. They were struggling and could be taken easily.

When he saw other animals crisscrossing the men's paths he got off his horse. These marks became more plentiful the further he traveled from the stream, the Lutheran knowing this was not the way, not these beasts and not these kinds. The tracks were overdeveloped and leaning heavy to the outside. The Lutheran grew cold with apprehension.

When the lance hit his horse the animal made no sound but fell instantly. The Lutheran brought the beast to the ground where he saw four more shafts buried no less than two feet deep, each placed mechanically with quick thuds. Instead of using the dead horse as breastworks he crawled through the darkness, crystals of ice plowing upward before him as he became the hunted.

Five wayward Indians coming off a month long drunk were mixing in the snow around him, amongst them a Comanche and Ute, a crazed Pueblan from the south with a brother who hated their Arapaho companion but had enough sense not to anger him. They'd left their families and tribes, running across one another in the great expanse of the west and that escape would be their downfall.

The Lutheran counted the footsteps of the Indians and smelled them as they looked for him in the moonlight. The first Pueblan stumbled while searching, not paying attention until he was found, the bounty hunter growing out of a snow bank to strike the man in the groin with a set of sawed antlers before backslashing so hard he was dead before losing the strength in his legs.

As he fell the Pueblan's brother sank an arrow in the leg of the Lutheran and ran, the Icelandic beast breaking off the shaft and pursuing him in deep snow with an onrush that changed the temperature in the air and left the last Pueblan with the shaft protruding from his chest. He then stood erect, craning his neck like a Doberman Pinscher to invite the others.

The Comanche, Ute and Arapaho youths watched the slaughter without moving. They were considering the Lutheran as something else besides human. More than a settler or white hunter or man of God, he was the interplay between hostility and a scream, the subject of stories but not real life.

This confusion gave the Lutheran time to move amongst them and as he did he positioned himself to be encircled before drawing his knife, restocking his other hand with the bloody antlers and urging them to do battle. He spoke to the men in Icelandic, knowing they would not talk amongst themselves from fear and why should man share language when there was so much obvious conflict to be tasted.

When they didn't move he did, disposing of each with his knife, the single finalizing strokes more snorts of sleepy death. They accepted what he brought, making no move to defend themselves, thinking the white was a man of mercy and forgiveness like the ones who prayed for them as savages in the A-shaped buildings of the towns they'd passed. Yet he turned them out brutally, their lives ending in a disgusting fashion as the last Arapaho considered never seeing the heat of summer or the change of fall. His mistake mistaking the Lutheran for easy prey.

Threadbare stood winded, the snow gathered around him in great red clumps, the spirits of the men rising skyward as their physical shells began touring back to the dust at his feet. He felt no remorse and little regret, wishing he'd taken the life of the postman for his carelessness around the rocks.

"Arrow," he said.

He walked back to where the Indians had found him and leaned against his dead horse, tearing away at his pants leg and cutting a ripe piece from the front of his thigh where the head of the arrow was buried. No change of expression came across his face, the procedure no more than another reason to continue.

As the night wore on he built a fire and boiled some water to clean it, taking the time to stitch and wrap the wound before doing the same to his torn pants. When finished he put the head of the arrow in his saddlebag with six others and agreed that their damage was inconsequential.

Disregarding his meeting with Conquin he considered finding another mount but decided to stay on foot, looking out at the mountains behind him as he stripped his horse of every last weapon and useful tool, making a sundry backpack from his saddle and riggings, one that reminded him of a fish pack from a childhood growing faint with the passing years.

The Lutheran began walking east, ready to give up on the money Dampier and Billy would bring until the fort fell completely silent and he could go in and take their identities in secret. But there was an anger in him that went beyond the pale cover of the new day, the clouds above gathering for a March storm that had come before he could invite it, new buds peeking through in places to ask if they could be part of nature yet or was their morning wine color an offense to the winter. And had the savages picked him out as a homesteader, somebody to be robbed and butchered so they could have another go at a week's refreshment?

As the question flooded over the Lutheran the face of the man Conquin reached out to smile at him, the deal having already been made and the authorities notified so Conquin could take full responsibility for Billy and Dampier's capture with a partial split of the money. Then the Lutheran saw the faces of the braves and did his geography, returning to their bodies to rifle through their pockets where he found ten dollar gold pieces newly minted and cold to the touch. A mile from the scene he discovered five horses that'd been fed and were renewed with vigor. They were branded with the insignia of the Missouri militia and each saddle had a rawhide bag full of liquor and smoke. The bodies of the horses were painted with the war stripes of each Indian except for two, the three he knew to be the death marks of the Comanche, Ute and the Arapaho. He took the horse of the Comanche and turned toward the fort with all the proof in the world that Conquin had sent the Indians to slaughter him.

18

"Do you want a little more before I have to go back down?"

"No, I need to stay up here today and watch to make sure those bloody savages bring his head back. You never know as much as they take to the bottle."

"They'll get him. They was five of them sons of bitches and one of him."

"Clarabelle get out of here before I kill you."

Clarabelle turned without saying a word and made her way down the stairs. The fort was still that day since most of the trustees had fallen ill except for three. Conquin's promise to take her with him after word of the Lutheran's exchange burned fresh in her mind. The word "honor" and "trustworthiness" was part of the mantra Conquin spilled, although Clarabelle only needed guidance as far as the nearest city for she'd formulated a plan to be done with him. As soon as they could mix with enough rawness to get Conquin off kilter she'd be free. What she could offer a man would be enough for them to kill for her and once there was news of his death she'd be gone. As for Dampier and Billy, they'd be finished when the Lutheran's head was delivered to Conquin.

It was all a smooth transition, one resting in the worrisome mind of Conquin as he stared out into the light waiting for the five horses to approach, switching his gaze from the east to the floor of the fort where Clarabelle was ascending to speak to the two new prisoners on the gallows.

"We're going to walk out of here just fine. Right under their noses without a word being said or a shot fired."

"Clarabelle, he'll shoot us dead just for you making fun," replied Dampier.

"How're we going to stroll out without musket balls in our heads Miss Clarabelle?" Billy was curious and more circumspect than Dampier. She saw deceit in Clarabelle's eyes and understood the game of the prostitute.

"Because Mr. Aten Mire Conquin has hired five of the meanest Indians known and they're out now collecting the blood of that Lutheran."

"That means fifty other people will be coming after us when, no, not when, if they manage to kill him. And that just adds more chips to the pot and makes our heads even more prized."

"No it don't Dampier."

"How," asked Billy.

"Because part of those fifty other people have got bounty out on the Lutheran and he won't have time to figure it out before he's dead. You've been traded for and your price has been bested so you ain't that important no more unless some renegade comes after you separate. Conquin offered to let you walk free as soon as he hears. It's worth a thousand plus for him and that's an unheard of sum."

"We'll see that day with shot in our brains," replied Billy.

"But these Indians?"

"Manson's out waiting to kill them as we speak. They'll be so drunk it won't take but five shots," said Clarabelle.

"Nothing works as smooth as that," replied Dampier.

As they spoke the small dark headed man with leech tattoos galloped out of the fort holding a tin cup of coffee. When he finished he pitched it onto the plains and took off at a sprint. He rode four miles and then dug in to catch the Indians coming along a small trail rising up from a trickling creek east of the fort. He'd sent them down the path and it would be the way they'd come back, if not with the Lutheran's body then all the better for he'd be the one to level the Icelander with a shot from Conquin's smoothbore, the gun having been loaned to him for half a day to finish either of the two tasks. Conquin had advised him on dealing with the savages.

"They'll be so besot with drink you can douse them five, four, three, two, one with a patient reload. I wouldn't even waste your pistol balls unless you're firing with frostbite good Manson."

He'd felt poorly and hadn't slept through the night, the vomiting lifting him from his pallet and emptying Manson so his once rotund gut shrunk back to his ribs, the cold of his stationary position behind a fallen tree enough to make Manson lie down and sleep forever but there was sound about and he should ready himself.

As the morning wore on he dozed, snatching his head up to look around every now and then before falling asleep once more. The racket coming from Mims Nickel had ceased in a few short days since most of the men had taken sick as the death pile grew.

Around noon he awoke to see a white rabbit but did not fire, instead rising to lay out a snare he carried in his tote for just such occasions. As he crawled back into position behind the tree he noticed there were circling footsteps around him but they didn't go in or out.

Manson cautiously got to his feet and readied himself to make a new post, accepting the fact that his laziness could've gotten him killed and even if one of the drunken savages managed to find him he could've been murdered. He heard no horses and no steps. It had all gone as smooth as the dreams he'd been spinning until now.

"I'll be damned, sure damned and done if I'm not careful."

Manson gathered his things and took them back to his horse, tying and retying as his shaking hands made knots that would not hold as a figure slipped into his place by the fallen tree and began watching him. Manson's eyes were darting around and he was looking for other cover but there was none, the one vacated being the best for what he would not get to finish. Manson wouldn't look where he needed to.

"Saddle won't pull tight. Why'd I take off the goddamned saddle?"

After a span of time too long for the hunter he leapt up onto his horse and began riding against the approach of the dead savages. The horse hopped with an apprehensive overkick and threw its head for the scent in the air was something dreaded, as if he'd caught cougar sweat in his nostrils, the smell closing then going back again, his heart quickening in his flanks as Manson became frightened.

"Goddamn animal! Cut that! They ain't no use in that!"

When the Lutheran stepped out in the pathway forty feet to his front Manson stopped and regarded him as lethal, pulling no barrel down in defense, instead he gulped and spoke.

"I'm glad you gave it to those drunk Injuns! They all need to go! I told Conquin myself if he thought they could get you he was wrong! I ain't got no fight left! I'll turn back!"

Manson's stomach rose up next to his fear and he vomited, taking his eyes off the Lutheran long enough for the man to step off the trail. When he looked up the bright vest of the Lutheran was hanging above a six foot lance driven into the dirt of the melting pathway. The sun broke from behind the clouds for a moment and blinded Manson who dismounted weakly, his legs going more to syrup with every effort, the stomach lining at his feet the last of his insides and the rest of his fill.

"Okay then you bastard, I'll take a shot."

And he was given one, clear and without any impediment as the Lutheran walked from cover in front of the vest and made his way towards Manson, his massive chest bared to the cold, shirtless from the waist up and shrieking a deafening cry echoing through the mountains.

The war club he carried was half the length of Manson's body and he swung it with two hands while walking, raising it slowly with all his rage as Manson fired the smoothbore and took out part of a shoulder that twitched with red tincture tissue but wasn't deep enough to slow him. The Lutheran came forward even faster.

When equal the length of the club to Manson's horse the animal tore away from the short man and ran, leaving Manson with the pistol and a knife. He delivered a quick cross slash tearing open the skin of the Lutheran's stomach but that was all as the bounty hunter waited for him to finish.

"Run," said the Lutheran.

But Manson was bold, not turning the gun on himself but stepping forward where he was allowed to put it against the head of the Lutheran before he was stricken a second later by Threadbare. The giant stove in the head of Manson with such force he caved into himself and bent at the waist, his bones going to powder and his mind back to hell. The gun went off as he did, firing into escaping clouds as Conquin listened to the second shot knowing two savages must be dead.

"He's done in a pair! That Manson is the man for the task! That morbid little Manson!"

19

Aten Mire Conquin never heard the horse of the Comanche as it rammed the front gate minutes later. He thought it was Dampier who'd taken up an axe to keep the fires going in the dying fort. There were only four left who had avoided the sickness as prisoners began to stumble across the plains in all directions, the plague fully investing itself and in control of all men.

The shoulder and head of a horse came into view but Conquin wouldn't acknowledge it until the massive door swung shut and the Lutheran was amongst them. The horse he'd rammed with was trotting about bloody and crazy sensing conflict with a cloudy blind eye but there was no opposition to be found.

The Lutheran rode over to a little boy stumbling with hunger and the child caught him by the foot, looking up at the half naked Icelander caked with the entrails of Manson. Without fear, cholera and death having stolen any sense he spoke.

"You it," the boy asked.

The Lutheran didn't answer until he caught wind of the child's fantasy.

"Leave when open," he said. "And the keeper?"

The child pointed to the roost of Conquin who'd seen the Lutheran and was calculating the impact of a leap to take his own life. As Threadbare gazed up the legs of the Comanche's horse buckled and he was on the ground, kicking the animal away from his body. Rolling over and standing he began whistling and corralling everyone from the fort but held Billy and Dampier still with his eye on the scaffold. The woman Clarabelle emerged from the caves to see if her feminine wiles might entice him but was slapped unconscious while straightening her rumpled dress and pushing her breasts upwards.

He grabbed one last child by the hair and slung him end over end out the front gate before turning to see what remained. Billy and Dampier were to his right on the gallows with Clarabelle crumpled on the fort's floor. Aten Mire Conquin was swilling booze in his perch and slipping into the poison of drink, the red of MIRE so bright the Lutheran thought him dreadful for writing such on his forehead. He could hear Conquin speaking to himself but his partners weren't listening.

The Lutheran turned and shut the heavy doors behind him, reburying the stakes with licks from the war club. He walked around waiting for the four rodents to escape, a few extra doors having been cut in Mims Nickel, the attitude being that its position was enough to deter any misbehavior on the part of the inhabitants, most of them dead or dying and that was in mere days. Those skeletons were now making their way to more hostile deaths throughout the countryside as the Lutheran let them have their temporal pass. Missouri being something put upon their graves but not a place to return to in their present conditions.

So he turned his attention, rolling out a kettle he'd collected from the inside of the fort. In it he put a mixture of grease from cooking, gunpowder, soil and what burned in the lamps they'd brought. The Lutheran had an idea of dynamite still four decades from patent and though he mixed it crude and without the proper ingredients he churned it to burn and burn it did, the walls of the fort going up so quickly in the dry air that within the hour he was forced to step back to see if something called out to him but nothing did. Threadbare the Lutheran watched, the flames running up and down the fort like fingers crawling on a wall, desperate ignitions knowing they'd burn no more once the crust was consumed.

And there was a memory in it for the bounty hunter, one of a school eaten by fire near Reykjavik. He'd been a child and as a child sleeping, within a quarter click of the school when it went up in the middle of a freezing night so close he could feel its heat, the flames over a hundred feet in the air and no chance to stop it. He recalled men dousing his house after carrying him into its courtyard, fire sprinting up the walls of the school and threatening his birthplace. Threadbare had watched the roof of his house smoke, the ice melting and falling in great pieces to the ground but still nobody approached the school.

He questioned whether it was a mother or a friend who returned him to bed, so young he barely had his legs but old enough to be left with the hound, a great dense animal that blanketed him from the heat and the smoking house like shade from the sun, the dryness from its fur rising and giving off the same scent of the fort before him.

The pounding had been going on for some time when the Lutheran came back from his memory. One of the great doors was moving back and forth and the stake he'd driven was threatening to break and it did. From behind it bolted a horse engulfed in flames, its body a color streak of orange burn, hidden from all else so it was not a horse but something bounding across the curve of the earth waiting to settle amongst flecking constellations.

"Kill it please," a voice said. "Could you help me a touch? I'd appreciate it since this is your doin."

The Lutheran turned. Behind him stood a man wearing the look of what was killing the fort. He was red headed and skinny to the bone but he had the equivalency of irritability that brings men to hate what they see if they suffer and that was not lost on the Lutheran.

"Name's Joe, Joe Potts from Alabama. That's my horse they let me bring with me for the sentence. Said they'd take a year off if I let 'em use it to pull the cart. You mind, I don't want him to die burnin up."

The horse was stealing snow with every imprint of its hooves, falling down to roll but still its hair was burning, the animal screaming when Threadbare came over the gaunt frame of Joe Potts and shoved a pistol to his chest.

"Put him down," he said.

"Likely best to use the big one sir. He's already kilt out like me so I don't see no reason to make it worse by aggravatin him with a goddamn pistol ball."

Joe Potts was adamant so the Lutheran gave him the same respect he gave others when he walked across their lands, pushing the length of his musket into the scrawny man's chest, the wind leaving his bosom with the impact and putting him back on the ground.

"Do I look like I can shoot that big son of a bitch? Put him down now! Do what you will!"

The Lutheran raised the barrel to the head of the man Potts then spun around and drove a ball between the eyes of the horse as it turned for some relief. It fell instantly, skidding to the ground and falling sideways fifteen steps from where they stood, lessening the distance as if it wanted to make a better target.

"Thanks, my wife and I appreciate your help. It was an awful strange way to get out of Mims Nickel but I'm out. I gotta go find her now. It's been three years and that's a mighty long time. That horse seen us and knew we'd do the right thing. They do that you know."

As he turned to walk away Threadbare watched him, every third step like the years of his sentence coming and going with missed footing, him like many of the convicts having no real idea how long they'd been held.

The Lutheran raised the pistol four times but did not fire, Joe Potts knowing he could be dropped without reason as the laws of brutality called for. On the fourth stay he turned a hundred yards away and held his arms out, pausing, delaying the hardship of life as if begging for termination but was rejected by the inhumane, the Lutheran refusing to kill the dying man whose course we cannot venture because he sits amongst the stars. Another unfortunate picked out for unspecified wrongdoing like a burning horse in a fort of plague.

20

Billy and Dampier saw the smoke but weren't present for the fire. They came off the gallows when the Lutheran shut the last of the doors and could hear his footsteps fading to the rear of the fort.

"He's gone," Billy said.

"No, but he's not in sight," replied Dampier.

Though they both doubted the sincerity of Clarabelle each stopped to help her, the slap she'd taken bringing her head cracking against a rock, her chest still. Dampier grabbed her feet and drug her down the tunnel leading to the cells. He left her there burrowed deep enough so no fire could find her if she wasn't dead already. When he turned away water was running down the side of the muddy wall onto her face and her color was fading to red where it dripped.

Aten Mire Conquin stood on the fort's wall intoxicated and walking a balance beam with a southward slant that could easily send him to his death. Billy saw him when they entered the caves, the heat of the fire embossing the MIRE like a brand on his forehead as he entrusted himself to extinction. The licking flames were up to his ankles and his leather boots were smoking but he would not come down from the post, holding up an espada ancha taken from the vaquero while screaming and praying in inebriated slurs to return to his island if for no other reason than not to be heard suffering. Billy saw him fall, but to which side she did not know. There was a flash of the short sword and then he screamed no more.

Dampier and Billy turned into their cell and stopped, the mud already falling from the walls and the heat building in the tunnel so both became dizzy. Smoke was being sucked by air deeper into the underground tunnels and Dampier noticed its movement.

"Billy, there's a way out the back!"

"I don't see nothing but mud and melting ice."

"This smoke is moving somewhere. It's going with the air. See it! Do you see it!"

"I do," she said calmly.

Dampier kicked at the lower wall and it was solid, grabbing Billy by the hand and pulling her out of the room where they ran into another barrier but one lighted enough so they could see the white haze of the burning fort rising over their heads and going up and over the wall. Smoke coated them in twisting columns and they went to their hands and knees coughing, both of them tearing at the bottom of the mud until finally Dampier pushed Billy to the top on his shoulders and she reached into yet another tunnel.

That was all it took, Conquin having had his fun by placing a paper thin obstruction so prisoners would think there was more when there was less. The wall Billy tore through was the entrance to the icehouse the keeper used solely for the cooling of his drinks and special meats. It was all a delicate maze that couldn't hold its own beyond a good booting or elevated temperature.

When they fell through the wall there was little ice remaining but it was enough to relieve burned skin. As they got to their feet a strange smile came across Billy's face. She could see sunlight through several boards in the room, the yellow streams of smoke mixing with the steam from the ice and what an aroma that was, for Billy and Dampier could've been anybody in their kitchen pulling noon baked pies from a Dutch oven instead of two lost pigeons in the confines of a crumbling fort.

"Son of a bitch, this rises to the outside," said Billy.

Dampier put his forearm through a small elevated window and the rotten wood splintered, putting them dirt level and outside the fort's wall. He immediately saw the fetlock joints of a gigantic horse so he pulled his arm in from the primitive grate, a short fence buried in the dirt so the prisoners wouldn't see Conquin's liquor stash delivered, further tempting even his own trustees to mutiny.

"This is it, we're going through here Billy."

"Lift me up and through. I'll take a look."

"No, he's out there circling."

Dampier put his face in the opening to see if the Lutheran had gone. He could see tracks but couldn't see whether he was lapping or turning eastward. He put his hand out in the slush and felt the heat of the burning fort, calculating the proximity of their exit to the hazard if there was a collapse.

"Goddamn Dampier! Just go! This smoke is rising by the minute!"

"If I crawl out and he's standing over me you'll be sorry."

"They ain't nothing between here and the settlements! I'll be more sorry standing by your rump choking to death!"

Billy pulled Dampier out of the hole and climbed past him when he tumbled back into the locker. She was summarily clutched and yanked backwards.

"Wait a damn minute Billy!"

"They ain't no minute to be had!"

She put her hands on her hips as he threw his body back into the opening. Dampier made his way into the slush on his elbows, coming out in the direction of the rocks Conquin had caught them in, the grate positioned so it looked like a natural rise near the stone quarry to its right though it was nowhere near it. Everything else was flat plain and a burning Mims Nickel, the blaze well on its way as several of the upright posts began falling outward to crash on the floor of the opening and catch fire to the dry grasses.

Dampier stood upright and when he did he saw the back of the Lutheran. He was riding a Percheron with a braided mane less than a mile out, the big draft horse running quickly northeast. He fell to his belly when the shimmering Threadbare turned but he met Billy in the hole and was ejected back onto the plain.

"Stay flat Billy. He's out there. I guess he's going on."

Billy put both arms out and her cheek to the earth, placing her hand on the shoulder of Dampier who was looking from bug level for a weapon. He saw a pistol resting in a black heap of snow fifteen feet away and began crawling to it cautiously, whispering to Billy to please keep an eye on the Lutheran.

"Go on, get it," she replied.

He didn't see the hand of the man gripping the weapon for he was put out on a downward slope. The place he'd died was a vantage point for shooting through the front gate of the fort but Dampier had no idea why he was there.

"It's one of the trustees. He's dead, it's his gun."

"He won't mind you borrowing it for a short while. He ain't got no use for it." Billy was watching his every move and also the moves of the Lutheran who'd dropped from sight on that measureless tundra.

Dampier wrested the weapon from the grip of the dead trustee and then checked him for shot. He was fully loaded, a rawhide bag of powder and ball enough for twenty plugs hanging from his neck. He thought the man a victim of the illness but he saw upon further inspection that the back of his head was caved in and one of his legs broken.

"You came too close," Dampier said to the dead man.

"Here he comes!"

When Billy screamed Dampier was slithering back but by the time he got there she took off for the rocks, crossing over him and begging him to run.

"He's seen us," said Dampier.

He came into clear view as soon as they were covered, gloomy and smudged, a look of menace and rage on his face, his body now fully painted with the stripes of the Comanche horse in some kind of mock respect for the hammering the dead beast had done on the gate of the fort. He was completely naked except for a set of rawhide moccasins, his body swirled and greased with a black and red paint that went down his frame in a snakelike spiraling until it met the top of his boots.

Though there was no saddle on the Percheron the Lutheran had started taking scalps and these hung in black, brown, red and white regalia around his waist in a putrid belt of absolute heinousness. Their grease the blood of humans staining his stinking body in the cold, the man Potts now a representative and lone figure for in the last hour the Lutheran had ridden down all of the escapees except for him, killing them one by one and racing their caps from their skulls, each watching as they died in anguish, the draft horse stamping out their final taps.

"Why'd you decide on such," Potts had asked.

"Tell the story of this day," replied the Lutheran.

Billy and Dampier's eyes were barely visible over the boulder they hid behind. They watched the Lutheran run towards the fort as if he'd forgotten something, ducking when the explosion knocked him off the animal and put him on his back, what was left of the standing fort quickly toppling with the blast of powder from the stored kegs by the butcher's pen.

The inburn made the area that much hotter so when Billy came from behind the rock to see the body of the Lutheran she did it with one hand to her face and her eyes in squint. Dampier followed her with the pistol, both frightened but needing to know he was dead.

"I have to see him," she said.

"Now's a good time. Nobody could've lived through that."

"You put one in him if he moves. He ain't an easy kill," she replied.

"He ain't going to move after taking that shot in the face straight on. He's done for."

Blood was coming from his eyes over the top of the mud paint to merge with another stream from his ears and nose. His face was totally black and there were small cuts in every part of his body. The scalps he'd excised were beside him in a great clump like a patchwork wig ready to be worn again. No breath came from the tremendous girth of his frame.

"My God," said Billy.

"Ain't no God in that lady. The devil's at your feet."

Billy grabbed the pistol and pulled back the drop over the firing pin, putting it to the chest of the Lutheran. Dampier snatched it away before she fired, repeating some verse from the Bible obscure enough for her not to violate an already deceased man.

"Desecration, not our place. Let the throne have the decision on this one. We ain't going to kill him no more than he already is Billy."

"He ain't getting no burial from me I tell you."

"We couldn't bury him if we wanted. Let's back out of this heat and go on. I bet Paterson will be glad to see us."

"We can catch them if we hurry. They ain't moving very fast I bet."

"If they're moving at all," replied Dampier.

The two turned away after checking for any sign of life with a bravery bordering insanity but there was none. With the brief respite from being prey they relieved themselves of the chase, for if the Lutheran lay in the midst of the fort having his life taken by chance, then they too could walk away knowing he'd no longer be in human form.

So they stepped into an hour they knew neither as early or late and he was left prone. As they strode away the Percheron got to his feet and ran past them bleeding. The animal stumbled once and then regained his strength, soon going out of sight in the rocks.

21

Clarabelle called three times but there was no answer. The back of her head was swollen and had a gash on it. She'd remained unconscious through most of the burning, the blast of the powder kegs turning the fire away from her as it made its way into the tunnels and through the timber doors. The flames were following the air of the opening Billy and Dampier had made with the grate, the ice and mud from the walls covering Clarabelle so thickly that when she awoke she was in darkness though there was a shaft of daylight on her. She had survived, insulated from the heat, the concussion she'd sustained healing in time if time were given.

She went out into the opening and saw that the once sturdy fort was now a pile of burning brush in several different stations. Pieces of its insides were strewn about and charred. A pool of grease smoked in suspension above the ground before her, its orange and black flames licking the crisp air of evening.

There were no bodies that she could see, only the grimy remnants of what people needed to live and work. Where the gallows had been now stood smoldering humps, their utility scorched and gone. A crow came across in the cold and the sun broke but Clarabelle didn't notice. She was walking to the post of Conquin but there was no post to approach.

"Conquin! Aten Mire Conquin!"

No answer, only the return of the bird seeking to settle without heights for perching.

"All gone, all done and gone," she said to herself.

Clarabelle made her way onto the plain and stood looking around, the pile of dead no longer visible. The thought of their fate left her feeling ill so she went to her knees to regurgitate, never noticing Conquin as he came from his hiding place beneath the ground, sounding a freedom he accepted with the destruction of the fort.

"Clarabelle! I dug this for just such an occasion. That or a visit from the savages, whichever came first."

"I thought you were dead." She looked over the streams from her mouth and nose but could not rise.

"No, no. I knew this bastard from front to back and prepared for every eventuality my dear. This was one such eventuality."

"I didn't expect anything like this to be eventual."

"Get up, get up! I've brought us a horse and some food I planted in oil skins not two weeks back in case this sickness spread. Of course I knew it would."

"You look good for a man burnt up." She got to her feet and wiped her mouth, Conquin bleary in her vision. He was in a suit of new clothes and polished boots.

"Hell woman, I've gone to the creek and bathed in the cold. Invigorating! I slid down in the bunker here after giving the Lutheran a show. He needed one, the dumb brute. Look."

Conquin had a cloth wrap he opened to reveal several nuggets of gold and a few small diamonds.

"My payment. Got it out myself. Took it from the governor's own safe a while back." Smiling Conquin shook them. "I'm sly Clarabelle. No more sly than when I'm crossed. The man hung for the robbery was personally exploited by me. It only took one word to the right politico and away I went. Did it during drinks and before dinner. He practically left it open for me to grab. Missouri owed me anyway."

"They don't suspect..."

"Why would they suspect a man so enthusiastic about this hellish task to need rocks? I'm untouchable. Lived through the fire just like you."

"Somebody drug me down the..."

"It doesn't matter how, you're out, through it and on the other side."

"I guess I am."

"I guess you are. Shall we."

"No Conquin, not yet. You know he's still out there."

"No he's not. He's gone on. He smelled the ruse and took action. He's a hundred miles distant by now. Got what he wanted and went about his business."

"This ain't been burning long enough for him to be a hundred miles distant."

"But it has my dear, two days and nights. I've been coming out late to make sure he wasn't around. He left after setting the fire and I promise you he has not returned."

"You were pretty goddamned drunk Conquin. I don't think you've seen much of anything but the hole you crawled in."

"Do you see him about?" He asked looking askance as if he were found out.

"No."

"So then, there we are."

"Conquin, I knew there was a reason why I should fall in love with you. And look there, the MIRE even lightened a bit."

They relaxed and walked amongst the embers of the fort that night. He opened a bottle of his best rum and they emptied it, Conquin taking two drinks to her one until they fell into one another's arms and made love by the fire, the white of their skin between each neck and hand shining in a moonlight darkened by clouds until there was no light at all.

When finished they forgot about dressing, rolling as close to the heat as their bodies would allow, both on the fringe of contentment as a man named Raxley

Hide was being buried thirty miles east by a friend who'd kept him on his feet for as long as he could until his legs twisted with weakness. His body became sick beyond its capacity to heal and finally after a climb back he fell, and then fell again. The second time he did not get up, his heart having starved to plunge no more.

Billy and Dampier tracked them through the melting snow, their imprints standing out like grins in war, the marks as obvious as a story in print, the drag and pull shuffle of Hide and Paterson a photograph of suffering. When they found them Paterson was sitting down the last stone on the grave in the dark. He said hello, offering the greeting of a man caught between fortune and friendliness, Paterson having done it right again, living by his nose while most refused to listen.

22

Aten Mire Conquin and the woman Clarabelle awoke to an early spring day. Their heads hurt but they were optimistic about the trip before them, knowing it could be anywhere and that direction was their choice. He even packed up everything, wrapping their bundles and strapping them to the small Palomino he'd hobbled, lifting Clarabelle into the saddle while he walked beside.

"We can trade for whatever you need Clarabelle. We'll run into more people if we head east."

His brogue was clear and confident, looking up as if she'd never been a whore but two notches more virtuous.

"Conquin, it looks like we were the only one's left standing here at Mims Nickel."

"Of course, that's the way it should be."

The snow came back in the afternoon but they were several miles away and picking up the pace, Conquin having jumped in the saddle to strike out on a trot lasting throughout the night. From time to time he'd turn back and smile at Clarabelle. She'd wink and they'd go on.

Snow and cold fell on Mims Nickel, a cold harmful to mortal man, the fires having all but quenched their thirst so no warmth could be found. And then there was that circling Percheron, a horse confused with the trauma of the blast and looking to have a feed, the temperatures dropping and hardening the ground so the grasses thickened with the exit of the sun.

At the coldest point of that midnight the horse stopped and circled no more. He was pulled over with a familiar clicking of teeth to stand next to a fire that burned so bright it phased out the chill. No one stood near it and the horse was alone, eating the grass close to the popping embers, its withers a shield for the man squatting on the tundra, reading the snowed over tracks of the recently departed. Absorbed, the Lutheran left the beast and walked with them, a bounty in his pocket proclaiming the governor of Missouri had a case to settle.

A Thing Tender

"What is it, about three hours before dawn?"

"Right about I guess. The sun'll be nice if there's any to be had today. It's been an awful October."

"It ain't October no more Dampier. Today's the first. She had them two just at the stroke of midnight, All Saints' Eve, we should eat a Druid when the dark one gets back to sleep."

"The Druids were a people Moba, not a vegetable."

"What the hell do I know. I'm just a midwife stuck out here on the plains. Ya'll the only business I've had since twenty five, how should I know a Druid ain't a vegetable."

"You ain't had no work in four years. How do you remember what to do?"

"I just keep clean rags and holler with the women. They do most of the work. Before I come across from South Carolina I done it three times a month, but out here ain't nobody to help. Do you see anybody gettin pregnant?"

"Well, not out here, but there's Mexicans to tend to."

"There's Mexicans everywhere, cause this is Mexico, but I ain't learned the talk and they'd just as soon use a priest or a pueblo sawbones. Ya'll would decide to settle on the west end of twenty thousand whites. You know this ain't Texas yet and it ain't never gonna be."

"We're here and we ain't leavin Moba. Now that the babies have come there ain't no reason to move Billy."

"Indians are gonna get ya, and if they don't the Mexican government will."

"There are other things to consider."

Billy had them in the fall of twenty nine about thirty seven minutes apart. The only help she asked for was from the midwife Moba Threnody, a sixty year old woman who'd ridden her donkey twenty two miles from the latterday settlement of Reckingfort Soo still several years from becoming the panhandle of a revolting Texas.

"Just time them Moba! Don't do a goddamned thing but time them when they come out to see who'll be the oldest! I can do the rest."

"They ain't two comin," she'd replied.

Moba did as she was told, Billy laying on a cot in a sod house south of the Punta de Agua with dirt in her hair and dust in her mouth. She'd grunted and cursed through a fourteen hour period as the twins moved around and positioned themselves in her body, the first son Torq coming out and then stopping, Moba reaching up to thump him on the head, the child crying before he could free himself from his mother, her fluid in his lungs and they'd started beating on him already.

"Oh hell in a firebush Billy, they's two of 'em!"

"I've been telling you that for the last hundred days but nobody listens anymore. I'm twice the size of me and these things generally don't weigh sixteen pounds apiece."

After Torq was liberated he was held up to Billy, the mother touching and kissing him, playing with his toes while Moba rubbed him with a towel. His body was the color of a new bruise and his eyes were yellow. There were questions of the sickness coming to take him but it never did, that conversation ceasing as quick as it started for there was another child on the way.

"Watch the timepiece. Is it wound Moba?"

Thirty seven minutes later the brother Latham fell out of Billy. She'd turned her head to get a drink of water and draw from her smoke and he came, hitting her with a sledgehammer pain as Moba squatted in the outhouse, Billy screaming for her to come catch him before he fell to the mud floor. He birthed himself and rolled into his mother, resting gently against her dilated privates, gasping before Billy reached down and strung him up with what strength she had left, popping his buttocks and bringing forth a wail. The first thing she noticed was that he glowed, his skin the shade of evaporated milk but only for fault of the light. She cut the umbilical and lay back just as Moba hit the door.

Dampier had missed it all, walking out to look at the prints of several Kiowa pony tracks as they circled closer and closer to his homestead. He could hear Billy screaming but was more worried about keeping them alive, their three years on the plain having been one hardship after another, all the first days drifting out and away from his memory.

The time at the fort and the pace they'd kept with the veteran Paterson had vanished but the morning Billy said the Lutheran could have them had not. She was tired of running so they stopped in the middle of the most hostile territory the west could claim and there they remained, so often seeing death they took turns sleeping, Billy's refusal to move closer to Reckingfort Soo pushing them to an early grave if they weren't careful.

When Dampier got back Billy was asleep. He picked up the twins, both looking at him curiously, the smoke from Moba's pipe irritating their nostrils and making them flex. The darker one Torq cried out while Latham tasted the smoke as if the habit were common to his first night on earth.

"That first'un is ugly as a starved beeve," said Moba.

"He ain't pretty," replied Dampier.

"They's other things to do besides be nice to look at."

"I'm sure he'll find them."

"She wasn't happy that you missed it."

"If we're dead ain't none of us going to be pleased."

"Them goddamned Kiowa's ain't touched me a comin out here. I got something for them when they do." Moba pulled a shillelagh from beneath the wooden chair she sat in and waved it at Dampier.

"You're going to let them get close enough to club?"

"I'll bash a sumbitches' head in. They'll look Moba in the eye afore' guttin her. I've had enough years of these flats anyhow."

"They don't want no old woman."

"They could steal my drink. I'm still a decent looking white too."

"You've had too many men."

"I married too many. They plum wore me out. The sixth one almost kilt me."

"Did it go smooth?"

"Babies comin outta mama's don't never go smooth."

"I'm going to lie down for an hour. Get me up if you think about it."

"Don't worry, that ugly baby will."

24

Someone said they saw him crossing the big river north of Juarez. Said they'd heard he was going down south to sit in the heat till something better came his way but they were lying. In the three years since he'd followed Dampier and Billy the Lutheran increased his pace considerably, traversing the Indian country and then back again, begging everybody from the Yakima to the Creek to send out their best so his blades wouldn't dull, but none of the brightly painted warriors would oblige.

In the spring of eighteen and twenty seven he turned on the settlers and the peaceful natives for free, leaving a trail of death and chaos from the Atlantic to the Pacific. He became a myth covering two thousand miles in a night, killing at will with no law sent forth to stop him. The Lutheran had gone insane and was now in the trade of murder, aching for the spectacle of the gruesome kill, all of man's earth his playground. Higher minds still wonder what happened.

One night a Ranger named Timms was sitting on the fluctuating border between the territory of Arkansas and Texas when he spotted the Lutheran cresting a hill, his horse dressed with so many heads that the clinking earbobs of the females and the beards of the men had become tangled, each as melted and fierce as the dread that'd severed them.

Timms could hear the man speaking in his native voice, wafting forth a song as soft as new snow. Before he got to his feet the Lutheran spotted him, spurring his horse, that same Percheron of legend as menacing as its rider, the summer soil turning up in cloves of dampness beneath its brick sized hooves. He dismounted at the fire and nodded to Timms. The Ranger offered him a seat and made no secret of pulling his weapons close.

"You know me," asked Threadbare.

"I heard of you, but I ain't lookin to take you in," replied Timms.

The Lutheran was covered in the scalps of humans, each one tied with a leather strap making more of a shawl than shirt. His face was greased completely red and there was no color to his eyes, some dye of ceremony having been put there to black them out. His stomach had been clawed by something he'd killed and its blood was on his chest, his arms on either side of it ashed out with a black so deep he looked to have no arms at all. His pants were the pants of his trade, the gore so prevalent that Timms walked away.

"Where you go?"

"I ain't got no fight with you Lutheran. You're not human and I ain't churched enough to challenge the devil. I'm dead if I stay here."

"Don't walk out of the light."

"Once more, I ain't got no rub with you. I'll go on."

"Nice man. Silly man. Weak man," replied Threadbare.

Timms walked until the firelight stopped blinking at his back and then he circled around, turning to see if the Lutheran would get to his feet but he didn't, the headhunter drawing even closer to light a cigarette hanging from his mouth. He stuck his face in the fire without thinking, one dull snake of a flame leaping forth and bringing the smoke to life.

"Ain't nothin good about this," said Timms.

As the night passed Timms would see his horse slaughtered and his gear gone through, every single item of his meager belongings slung out onto the prairie, some blowing past him a quarter mile out.

"He ain't gonna do right by me. He's in it for the ugly," the man mumbled.

When Timms had all he could take he packed his pistol and began walking back to the fire, its size doubled with the burning carcass of his horse. The Lutheran had built a spit with lashing from his saddle and was roasting the flanks of the animal as the Percheron kicked its head about like a ball, bloodying the grasses with every roll.

"Ranger's back," said the Lutheran.

"I aim to kill you Threadbare cause I can't take you in. There's more paper on you in the territory than a man could read so you ain't worth jailin. I'm damn sorry you've gone bad. You made a decent lawman once."

"And your wife?"

"Don't do that, cause I won't make this fair," replied Timms.

"She'll die after you, then your kids Timms. Timms from Duckett."

With no intention of asking for surrender Timms raised the pistol and fired, the ball going into the shoulder of the Lutheran as Timms cursed himself for not stepping closer, few men having had such an opportunity with the mobile killer.

"A dent," said the Lutheran, his black eyes every pit and dark recess known.

Timms was reloading when the Percheron leveled him, galloping over the man to break his jaw and a leg, turning back before the Lutheran stopped him.

"Tiny Timms," said the Lutheran.

Nudging the horse to the side Threadbare went over to kick Timms's shoulder until it broke. One shot, then two, reaching down to turn his face to the fire so he could watch.

Threadbare sat in the dirt and pulled out his knife, a caramel colored poker taken from a trapper in the north woods. The ball had lodged in the muscle of his left shoulder and as he leaned forward Timms could see what he meant to do. Without heating the blade he cut a hole around the wound and put his finger in it to slow the bleeding. He then dug into his own flesh until the ball was removed, Threadbare popping it into his mouth for cleaning before hammering out a more acceptable shape with the brunt of his blade.

"Not the first," said the Lutheran.

"I'll do it," slurred Timms. "If I'm goin it ain't gonna be with me watchin."

"My pleasure," replied the Lutheran.

As Threadbare got to his feet Timms began looking around for something to defend himself with. All he could find were lumps of wire grass and his own shooter, the gun now in the hands of another reloaded with the very ball he'd shot.

When the Lutheran was ready, blood seeping from the hole in his shoulder, he went over and pulled a Long Tom rifle from his pack and gave it to Timms, placing his hands on it so he could fire when ready. The Lutheran then turned his back, Timms so shocked that the instinct of survival ground to a halt in his reeling head.

"I ain't playin no more Lutheran!"

"No games left," replied Threadbare.

The Lutheran walked off fourteen paces, spun around and held both arms out. Timms waited, then swung the Long Tom up and shot, the miss throwing up dirt by the fire nowhere near his target.

"I gave time," said the Lutheran.

Timms didn't respond as the mass stepped into the night and left the man lying immobile in the circle of the glow. Nothing was said and dawn came, the Percheron and the Lutheran having disappeared from sight.

Timms fed the fire until it brought a group of eight buffalo hunters over to hear the story. They listened, later that night all of them dying with Timms's own pistol, not a single one hearing another's death. Timms would be last, seeing the Lutheran smile at him before his eyes were shut from life like replica dark.

25

Moba had her stroke two years after the boys were born so they took her into Reckingfort Soo to rip the side out of her hovel and load all her possessions in the back, the woman having built the house around them. Moba sat stoically as they traveled, accepting no extra compassion and asking for nothing other than respect. She was being taken in by the Mox's but failing to do her part was unacceptable.

Black headed Torq thought it was funny to pull up the wheel brake so he did it again and again as Billy worked, looking at his mother to see how much she could take. At first Billy was patient then snapped, jerking him from the seat by the hair before beating him with his own shoe. Latham watched the incident and said nothing, crawling into the lap of Moba who sat taking inventory with a half frozen mouth and numbed left arm on the back of the wagon. Repulsive to Torq, she was a figure of security for the timid Latham.

"You ladies best pack it up and tell that Dampier his cattle won't make it through the summer."

Billy turned to look down the row of twenty small houses, twelve of them having been emptied since the Texans began making war in Mexican territory three hundred miles southeast of Reckingfort Soo. The southern government was bent on making life difficult for the settlers since revolt was on the horizon.

"We'll pay you no mind pastor. Go on about your running and don't stop till you hit New York," said Billy.

Moba heard the man first and was pounding her good hand on the side of the wagon through Billy's response, unable to bring forth the curses she was thinking.

"They're paying the Comanche to set the grass on fire when the drought hits in August. And it'll burn Billy Mox. You stay out there and you'll burn too."

"Rumors! They ain't killed us yet! Besides, the Comanche hate the Mexicans. We give them a cow or two and they'll be fine. As long as the Comanche and Kiowa can trade they won't harm us. You make them bad with your talk when they ain't."

"The Mexicans pay better than you and they pay big. There's enough renegades and crazies to kill all of you and five years of luck don't mean..."

"Shut up," screamed Moba.

Latham began to cry and crawled out of her lap, meeting his brooding brother next to a cornhusk lamp, the smaller Torq waiting on him with a palm full of oil for his red black hair. It ran into Latham's eyes and sent Billy into hysterics. She turned on the preacher who sat astride a Paint ready to turn eastward.

"Moba, pull those two apart goddammit! Listen reverend, Dampier's finally turned into a decent cowhand and we've just managed to store enough for winter the last two years. We ain't busting the eastern banks with deposits but we ain't dying, so go on about your business and tell Sam Houston there's plenty of room out here if they'll come. Until then, we're waiting for the lease to come through and..."

"That was a hoax Billy! Mexico wants you Catholic and speaking Spanish or you'll be evicted!"

The pastor's horse was throwing its head in defiance but the man held tight, the animal sidestepping and waiting for a chance to launch him.

"Still we'll wait and see if the province will grant it. They ain't run off the Apache, Comanche, Kiowa or Papago, so I don't expect we're in line for eviction."

"That's because three of those tribes have eaten at least five hundred Mexican militia this year alone!"

"Reverend, they don't eat human flesh!"

"That husband of yours kills too many of their buffs or forgets to pay his toll and you'll see different missy! All it takes is one drunk Indian to ruin a family. I hope your kids are prepared to be main dishes or sword practice for that bunch of drunks in Chihuahua!"

Moba limped behind the man's mount on one leg as he spoke, the pastor so infuriated he ignored the crippled old woman. When she threw her pipe tobacco on a rub behind his horse's saddle it was enough to throw him, the man's eyes looking up from the dusty street as Moba repacked her pipe and smiled at the boys who were looking over the edge of the wagon.

"Yes shrrr," she said.

"And thanks for signing the certificate padre. People really need to be married in a church to have little ones like these. But maybe next time," Billy added.

26

By September there were only two families left in Reckingfort Soo. Both believed it was by order of Mexico's provincial governor that the smoke began to rise north of the Canadian River but they were wrong. Nature had done the task, knocking a Kiowa brave off his horse with a lighting bolt so dry and quick that it killed him from a bright blue sky, the body of he and his horse smoldering before catching fire to the water starved prairie. The wind took over from there and before long a blaze the size of five city blocks was burning between two rivers and squaring outward towards the settlement.

Three Comanche's fishing on the Punta de Agua twenty five miles north saw the smoke in the early evening. They rode at a fierce pace to the head of the fire and then back, sweeping through Dampier's homestead to turn a herd of two hundred buffalo into a larger one of a thousand moving west.

Dampier was sitting on his horse fearing the worst when they passed, one of them in a pair of white man's boots clucking twice from his throat and then throwing his chin at the smoke. He knew what they'd do if it were their own, having seen them pull up their stakes and move an entire camp of five hundred within an hour so agile was the troop.

But he was grounded and in the midst of a hundred head of cattle that stamped with the exit of the buffalo, the braves hounding them without mercy as some of the bulls darted out to challenge their mounts but were soon turned back. There was a slight mix of bovine and brawn when they crossed but Dampier's steers were cut out by the Indians, the buffalo displacing the cattle like man through child.

Billy came in sight just as he got the cows moving back towards the rickety lot next to her garden. She was riding Moba's donkey and waving her hand, the animal's ears bouncing up and down like wings, aiding the cumbersome beast no more in its pace.

The cattle picked up the scent of the smoke and began turning towards water. Dampier allowed them to drift north over the plains as Billy rode up.

"Moba says..."

"Come in closer Billy! I can't hear you!"

She continued to scream out, the blather of the retreating cattle drowning her effort until Billy was next to him.

"Are the kids with Moba?" Dampier's face was worried, expecting a loss greater than the small herd.

"She says you should ask them to help you Dampier!"

"They're Comanche Billy!"

"We ain't got enough arms to stop it and Moba says they know how. They been doing it for a thousand years!"

Dampier turned to look over his shoulder. In the distance he could see the last of the braves grinding their unsaddled ponies with gaping legs naked to the thigh, each man's hair lifting to form a set of dark blue horns as they rode, their manes falling back before spiking again.

"Welcome to the plains," he said.

"We got most of it down by now," replied Billy. "But it won't matter much if it all burns."

What they see. A line of smoke to the south with so much fire in its stomach that no fire shows at all. The sun is setting in the west, its obscured temperament less vicious with a coating of white, the wind blowing it back and forth across the great red ball like a boy passing before you in a furnace lit room.

The flames raze everything and move on northward, the grass nothing more than a pathway for what it's done since before man had a beating heart. It sees the house and the lot that Dampier built and it can hear the children screaming inside, the man kicking in the front door not their father or a familiar as the black headed one holds his leg and bites down to protect. He's a big pale beast who pulls out the elder Moba but she will not answer, grunting up to him like his head is in the clouds. The man draws a knife and then tosses her aside, walking into the house where the children fall silent. The fire sees his white hair and shirt of scars. It thinks he would be a difficult carcass to burn so it moves on.

Attention is pulled away as the Comanche with the help of Billy and Dampier sweep before the red talons of the blaze dropping torches. The flames collide along a five mile path and dam up the intent, smashing the fire with its own power, diminishing the grassy fodder throughout the night. Finally, there's nothing left of the fury.

The Comanche and the Mox's ride back and forth along the route of the blight not speaking to one another. The braves think the whites should've let it be this time, but they don't understand acts of God and never will.

"It's burned its own self out," said Billy.

The Comanche did not answer. Looking, they were circling their horses and whistling back and forth.

"They think you're funny on the donkey," said Dampier.

"Well I guess I've done my share in the last few hours. They can laugh if they want."

The Comanche spoke amongst themselves and then stopped, thirty of them now watching east and west as fires grew up and died. They seemed to have no need to ride the line once the medicine was administered.

"It went right up to the farm but I didn't have time to stick my head in when I passed. Did you?"

"No Billy, but Moba will do the right thing if it came to getting Torq and Latham out. If not, one of these men probably did."

As Billy and Dampier discussed the tenacity of the Comanche the riders rode off without saying a word. One of the younger ones came back to tap Dampier on the shoulder and ask him a question.

"I don't know what you're saying," said Dampier.

Just before they both became disgusted with the language barrier an older Comanche wearing the cape of a Mexican officer came out of the dark and spoke.

"Horse big," he said. "You have horse big?"

"Just this one."

He motioned for Dampier and Billy to follow him, riding within a mile of their homestead where the men dismounted to look at the ground while Billy's donkey fell behind. She was enveloped in smoke but could hear the men's voices. Several small gaming birds flew against the direction of the stale mist filling her lungs and she jumped when they lit up and crossed over her.

There was no moon for such a clear night, the fire having doused the purity of the plains making their vastness less pronounced. Before she knew it Billy was boxed in and lost in the smoke, feeling inferior for having been behind them one minute and gone the next.

"Who is it? Hello!"

But there was no announcement, the figure coming up and over her just as Dampier looked down at the track of the Percheron in the burnt grass.

"Billy," he said. She did not answer.

27

Dampier hit the door of the sod house at a full gallop with his pistol drawn, his horse skidding sideways, the impact of the strike enough to take the door off and collapse the mud bricks above the entryway, the light of morning falling into an empty home no more disturbed than when he left it the day before. He jumps off the animal and shoves it away, standing with his back to the wall meaning to surprise an intruder that already knows he's there.

"Moba!"

There's no response so he moves a little at a time, short dusty steps as his horse walks around to the back of the house and begins drinking from a bucket, the slurping making Dampier tense.

"If you've got them in there Lutheran just come on out! They ain't done a thing but be born and that ain't no count to kill them!"

He looks into the house, seeing the corner of a cot in the back of the room. There's a jug of whiskey he picked up from a skinner on its side and it's dripping on the floor from the table. A glass sits beside it half full with Moba's pipe stem growing from the oily liquid. There's no sound except for the drinking horse.

"I'm stepping in," he says. "They ain't no reason for anymore to be kilt!"

He goes in with the mouth of the pistol up over his head, bringing it to the center of his body with a long stride, squatting and moving his frame like a turret to find both his sons sitting placidly on the cot leaning against feather pillows. Latham's asleep but Torq is just staring, his eyes finding his father before pointing out the window.

"Pop," Torq says. "Him gone, take Mama Moba."

Dampier rushes over and picks them up. Latham moans and begins crying, his back wet with sweat, the sun coming in on his hair and stopping on the shoulder of Torq. He's blinking, strangely set in defense of what has gone before him.

"Big white man with cluck like the Coo-manch pop. See him give me mark for good boy. Not mean to me. Him say mean Latham but not mean Torq."

Dampier walked them both outside and then panicked. He looked out on the plain and could see the lines of smoke and feel the heat growing with the morning air but there was no Billy and no Moba.

When he held the kids up Torq reared back and punched Latham in the face, his wail so loud that Dampier put Torq on the ground and lifted him off the dirt with a slap to his bottom. He fell on his face, then got up and turned without saying a word, sniffling slightly and that's when Dampier saw the dressing.

"Latham, play with the chickens, I've got to have a look at your brother."

The mark was in the middle of the boy's back covered with a cloth patch. Torq didn't become frightened until it was ripped off, squirming around so Dampier had to sit on the boy's legs to keep him still. The letters were an inch tall, having been done with the ink the Apache use to color their horses permanently about the face where the bone doesn't flex. The word LOST was embossed there, its letters black and as symmetrical as if they'd been written in stencil.

"Him say he know daddy. Him hard to hear," said Torq.

Latham chased a chicken through the door and the animal went over the bed, one of its claws falling on the skin of Torq's back and scratching him. Torq jumped up and ran the bird into the yard. A minute later Latham came in and said he'd killed it. Dampier didn't reply.

28

Threadbare drug Moba for a quarter of a mile before dealing with her. They went past several Comanche striking counter fires, the Lutheran being as stealthy as they when it came to hiding on the plains. He stood completely still when the braves were close, the woman at his wrist still unconscious from the lick he'd given her with the handle of the big knife. The two were nothing more than inexplicable shadows on that dark and rolling waste. Knowing or not, the Comanche went on.

Billy came within a few yards on her donkey but Threadbare didn't have enough respect to stop his dragging, the smoke and the night enough to black him out as he towed her babysitter for punishment, promising himself that Billy would be next.

Moba awoke with the Lutheran straddling her, the woman opening her eyes to see a picture of everything that came after death but not before. She knew she'd be answering for certain mistakes in her life, her stroke the very hand of God himself, but death couldn't be this vindictive. It had white hair that fell to her face and it looked at her with black eyes, running the tip of its finger down the bridge of her nose while dressed in the wares of so many tribes she couldn't name them. On its face was a painting that appeared to be a fanned deck of cards but was more a map of purgatory. His weight was taking Moba's breath, his stinking mouth offering something in the language of the Comanche but it was too ugly to answer. Then he came through.

"Time now old woman. I used to see old woman cross from the Soo. I gave you more days. I'm the giver and you'll thank me."

"Do what you will."

Moba spoke and then closed her eyes, the woman's heart stalling before picking back up again. She thought of all her husbands and saw their faces, even the ones that beat her and ran around drunk with the whores of every frontier city.

"Forgiveness," she uttered.

In her thoughts she sat with Edgar, her third, drinking bourbon under a Bald Cypress in the last of the bayous before you stepped into the colony of Texas. They watched the brown pelicans dip into the murky water and slapped mosquitoes on their arms, the liquor warming them into affection as he made love to her before going into the territory and not returning.

She couldn't think of where she went after that but there was always some-body loving her in their own peculiar way. Always a hand touching her face or a man to bury and what is living if not expecting things to end. Now the Lutheran had brought such an ending.

"Do what you will," she said again, her slur cured for the moment, Moba's tone clear.

The Lutheran got up and watched the Mox's and the Comanche as they fought against nature, knowing he was as much of a force as any fire or flood or gun brandishing roughneck. He loosened from his body anything less natural than his own flesh, dropping his gun and knife to the ground, deciding this one would be quiet like the old days.

Bending at the knees he repositioned himself on top of Moba, enclosing his hands around her throat to find that the woman had passed. Moba was looking up at him and in that gaze was a foreshadowing of a beast even more horrible than the Lutheran. Offended, he drug her in circles until her back bled and then turned his attention to the rest of his work, his chest drawing in voluminous clouds of smoke.

29

The blow knocking Billy off the donkey wasn't enough to kill her so she fought for as long as she could, the emptiness not hitting back until she'd tired herself out. Gasping, she was struck from behind as soon as her hands fell in sub-mission.

Her face was blinded by the blood pouring from the top of her head. When she turned to match the footsteps with the figure it hit her across the mouth. The bludgeoner looked down at her face and rolled Billy over so she wouldn't choke. She said "you're with him" and then it all went liquid black.

There was bouncing throughout the day but she never saw anything more than grassy plains beneath the donkey. It didn't seem to be led by anyone and she couldn't hear another horse but Billy continued to play dead for the benefit of her captor.

She'd loosened her bindings by the late afternoon, Billy still able to smell the smoke from the fires in the collar of her shirt. The sleeves had been pushed down beneath her wrists and that'd given her enough leverage to slide them free with her thumbs bent. Her hands broke apart behind her back as she tipped forward and fell on her shoulder. The bone cracked with the impact and made her stomach hurt. Shaking her head from side to side she cleared her vision and got to her feet.

Moba's donkey was staring at Billy so she gently pulled its ear. The animal had been following a game trail that cut northwest from Reckingfort Soo, choosing the quickest path away from the fires as soon as it heard no human voice, the cargo of Billy on its back nothing more than something to carry that wasn't speaking. The instinct of survival had sent it on an eleven hour march and now Billy was a day away from the homestead.

"I should've just looked up and got off," she said.

There'd been no change in the terrain but she had crossed a shallow river because the donkey's legs were wet to the knees. The bag of the jenny was full and Billy had a terrible thirst so she squeezed a teat until it gave a slight flow. Billy filled her hand as much as she could and then drank, the jenny stepping sideways when she touched a fresh bleeding bite mark next to its tail.

"Oh hell," said Billy. "What did this?"

Billy looked down at the ground and froze as the donkey took three steps forward, shuddered and ran. She stayed on her hands and knees knowing what she'd see but did nothing until the Long Tom rang out. A low throaty rumble came from the lungs of the jenny and a second later there was another shot followed by a thump.

"Go on you son of a bitch! If you've killed my husband and kids then I guess I'm next!"

She continued to hold herself down with handfuls of grass until ready, suddenly coming up ramrod straight but there was nothing there. The donkey lay dead two hundred feet away, a shot having gone in the back of its head and another on the side. She saw Threadbare sitting north of her, his outline distinguishable by the width of his shoulders and the smell that followed. He had his hand in the air and was waving her in his direction.

With no other play Billy walked up the game trail until she was close enough to see the contempt in his face. That's when the Apache sprang from the grass beside her and hit her squarely in the back of the neck, knocking Billy to the ground once more, her body falling limp on the worn path.

30

There were words in Athapascan she could understand but the ones the Apache were speaking to the Lutheran were jumbled, the licks she'd taken in the last day enough to rearrange her sense of any tongue. Her hands were once again tied and she was aloft on stilts amongst other structures of the same height. Billy lifted her legs but they were bound also.

"No price," the Apache said.

"None," replied the Lutheran.

When the Apache spoke English she turned her head to follow him, the man walking out to look at Billy one last time before he left. His black hair had been cut short and he wore the hide pants of a white hunter. As he peered up Billy could see he bore the scars of the Sun Dance on his chest and that he'd gone out as a boy into the desolation to sacrifice two of his fingers to the great Power but he'd not been rewarded.

"I'll pay triple," said the Apache.

"No," replied Threadbare.

The man had come to the burial ground to blaspheme the Comanche, refusing to forgive them for the rape of his sister after the Comanche and the Apache clashed over a herd of bison two springs before. When he took it upon himself to go out and kill two Comanche warriors without consulting his father he became an outcast and had wandered the plains since without mission or purpose, his skill and deviance going up for the best bid. It was comical for the Apache renegade to know that white flesh would be dying on the Comanche's sacred soil if he couldn't purchase her.

He'd collected pure gold from the Lutheran just for following a donkey but he knew the white woman's loins would be more valuable for bartering. Yet, he was also smart enough to realize that the reputation of the Lutheran had been earned and that you had to touch him to believe he was real. Any man with such a presence was not to be harassed.

There were other exchanges as the Apache urinated on the poles of Billy's makeshift tomb. She looked about and could see the bones of others, their beds of slat built sturdy against the plain's winds. The sun and the buzzards had destroyed their physical bodies and as they drifted into the afterlife they could see her pale skin living beneath them. She'd become a desecration, a tool of vengeance for a belligerent Apache gone bad.

Billy listened to the clinking of the coins then saw the Apache get on his horse and begin riding northwest. There was no more movement until she heard the Percheron snort and saw the head of the Lutheran come up over the side of her body standing on the back of the horse. He kept his eyes turned away and wouldn't look at her as he climbed.

"Bad Indian. Billy's so high in the sky," he said.

A slat broke beneath the weight of his hand and he went through but caught himself, a splinter as long as a finger going into his wrist. The Lutheran took it out with his teeth and spit it in Billy's face before standing over her on the burial altar. The poles quivered beneath him but he got back down as quickly as he'd come up. The Lutheran's body bent like a washrag and he was on the ground before she could blink.

When he returned he'd moved the big draft horse around where he could see the Apache. The Lutheran stood in the saddle until the animal settled, cooing to it like he was speaking to a child. He then placed the barrel of the Long Tom across her midriff and spoke.

"Don't move Billy." Then he looked down. "Don't move horse."

He used Billy's womb for a brace and then tilted his weapon up slightly, his rank wind rising from her privates and coating Billy's face as he grooved into the stock. The opening of the enormous rifle was six inches from her left cheek so she turned her head away and took a deep breath just as he fired, the discharge knocking the Apache from his horse, the man a falling dot on the plain.

The Apache's horse bolted backwards and the Lutheran waited for it to cut the distance before he shot again, the animal dropping in a great heap with little drama. The Apache got up stumbling, falling again as the Lutheran poured a sip of water in Billy's mouth and dropped down on the Percheron to go cut the man's throat and collect his coins.

"Dead red! Dead red," he called.

Billy watched him depart over her swollen shoulder, his words garbled in her ear from the rifle's report. When the sound of the Percheron's hooves faded she let her head flop and begged the silence for a reprieve.

31

Dampier didn't leave the kids in Reckingfort Soo because there wasn't time. He'd barely missed being destroyed by the fire and now his wife and Moba were missing. He knew the boys would see bleaker outcomes in this life so why not expose them to the obvious.

Both Torq and Latham sat and watched him in the little sod house, each asking questions about the women in their lives and where they'd gone. Most of the day had passed and he still hadn't made a decision about which way to strike out. He questioned himself whether the Comanche that'd help him divert the fire could've also reeked havoc on his quiet life, but he knew if they wanted him off the plain they could've easily set the fires themselves and burned everything he'd built. They'd circled the place for years now and he'd done everything rumored to keep them clear of his family. If they wanted Billy or the kids they would've taken them already.

Dampier picked up the track just behind the house. There were blood smears every few feet so he followed them while Torq and Latham walked behind, all three finding the body of Moba where it lay broken and partially eaten by coyotes.

"Moba," said Latham.

"Her unawaked," replied Torq.

Dampier was surprised neither recoiled from the gruesome sight. Torq went over with a zest for the macabre and squatted down with his little boy confusion to try and wake her but she didn't respond, her eyes staring blankly into his face. Finally the smell chased him into his father's arms but Dampier wouldn't pick him up.

"We got to put her under boys. Dig a hole and rock it up. It's what you do."

"Dig a hole and rock it up," repeated Latham.

"It's what you do," added Torq.

They walked back and got a potato pick and a shovel, all three of them returning to put Moba in the ground next to where she lay, no other ceremony given except for a simple prayer by Latham.

"It ain't deep enough," said Torq.

"It's all we got time for boy. Talk to God. One of you talk to God," said Dampier.

Latham reached down and picked up a handful of dirt. When he threw it into the air it spread out and came back against the body of his father.

"Go back mama Moba. Go back to Jesus," said Latham.

Dampier stood over the grave and felt his faith draining. At times he missed his own pursuit of pure pleasure and the fact that he'd enjoyed killing when he had the chance. As a missionary he'd been a novelty, but there was a reason he was always comfortable around sin.

"Let's go now. We're done here," he said.

Both kids jumped into the unhitched wagon when they got back to the house but he told them to get off. He'd traded the Kiowa a week's meat for a travois in the first days when they'd arrived and he meant to put it to use, its tracks easily blending with a hundred other tribes on the prairie if somebody followed. The sled was leaning up against the house and hadn't been touched, its body made from firm oak and the flesh of mule deer.

"Torq, Latham. Go around and bring that travois over here. The thing you pull behind the horse."

"We're too little. It too heavy," said Latham.

"Me three. Almost three," added Torq.

"You two lack a little strength. But if you can walk, you can carry," Dampier responded.

They managed to get it moving while Dampier packed every weapon he owned. Moba had bought a firearm from a gunsmith who left after fifteen days in Reckingfort Soo. After a week of black ice and no business he was giving away his skill so Moba took advantage, having him forge a .52 caliber pistol that was more of a musket weighing seven pounds. The gun was fashioned from so much iron you had to holster it on your animal and make sure you hit where you aimed. Reloading was more dangerous than being struck by the hand cannon. But if you were touched, you were downed.

The boys stopped feeding off their father's worry when the travois was hooked to the horse and they were allowed to climb aboard. Torq began bouncing up and down while Latham was watching the animal drop its waste, the dung barely missing the downslide of the travois before falling to the ground.

Dampier made a couple of turns until he guessed the route of the track. It'd been made in a blatant fashion and even Torq picked it up, the disarranged soil an invitation more than a puzzle. As he began to follow he looked back one last time.

"Boys, make sure that satchel don't come off or we won't eat. You'll be left if you hit the ground because I ain't watching. It's mean out here and it's gonna get meaner."

The boy's faces were filled with dust then they toughened, looking out on the prairie as their father made his way north to intersect a gaming trail that snaked out of Reckingfort Soo. What piety he had left was loosening in his chest like a summer cough and he knew he was ready to kill again.

32

"It'll take more than this to make me quit! You can leave me out here for eternity but I ain't dying till I get ready so you better do the killing yourself and get it over with!"

Billy couldn't stop thinking the Lutheran had gone after the children or was in wait somewhere for Dampier. Her wrists and hands were weeping a clear fluid and she'd begun to get a fever but would not close her eyes.

Sometime during the night Billy heard Threadbare drag the body of the dead Apache underneath her. He entered at her feet so she couldn't see him, the heels of the warrior breaking the reeds of grass in concert with the easy working grunts of the Lutheran.

"You ain't striking a bit of fear in me you pale bastard! Goddamn you to the hell you came from! You kill from afar like a coward!"

"Mmm and close." The reply came from somewhere undetectable and made her shiver.

In the early morning Billy passed out from exhaustion and when she awoke her clothes had been cut away and strewn about on the ground. He'd pulled the fabric down through the slats and slit it in strips until Billy was completely disrobed. She moved her hips back and forth but there was no soreness, the man having no interest in rape, murder and humiliation his preferred method.

Looking to the east she could see the cranial lift of the sun as it spread over the prairie and began to dry the dew on her skin. The smoke was rising off her stomach and heating the fresh blood of her wounds that'd coagulated throughout the night. Her heart was beating in her throat and her lashings had been retightened.

"Will it ever stop," she said to herself.

Billy didn't see the head of the Apache until she looked away from the burning ball of the sun. It was hanging next to her left wrist, the carrion of the neck touching her fingers when she flexed them. The black eyes of the Indian were looking at her lifelessly. His scalp had been taken to adorn the pole near her other hand but she didn't notice until she was told.

"A gift," said a voice.

The Lutheran had removed the corpse of a fifteen year old Comanche brave gored by a Spanish bull. He'd made himself a bed on the vacated burial rise and was lying on his chest watching Billy struggle and pull away from the head. The Percheron was looking up at his master as the base of the poles began to split with the Lutheran's weight. Equal in height he gently spoke to Billy, his heavily accented voice like a thumping drum.

"I marked the little one. The black. Turk?"

"Don't say his name! Never say my boy's name!"

"Torq. I marked Torq for killing Billy. I'll come for Torq."

"Torq'll come for you."

"No man comes for Threadbare." He was struggling to get the words out and stalling between syllables, pulling them from his mind like reciting something memorized as a child.

"That Torq. That Torq will leave Billy for whores and money. Torq come from Billy first and will go even quicker."

"Then fix it so I don't have to see him leave. Let me go or do me in."

"Threadbare will take all Mox's when the time comes."

When she stopped answering he stopped casting his lurid eyes upon her, throwing his legs off the side to dangle them in the air before jumping to the ground without the aid of the horse. Threadbare stood looking around at the feathers as they blew in the wind, the graves dressed accordingly depending on the years and accomplishments of the person who'd been lifted to the heavens.

In all there were thirty beds spaced eight steps apart. What the great spirit saw from above was four rows of five bodies with the eldest of the tribe in the dead center breaking the square in two, his ashes having rolled and tumbled to the western sea fifty years before. Around the outer edge were the tombs of eight warriors built in a circle to protect the middle. Billy was on a southernmost rise in a grave out of proportion by its placement.

The Lutheran waited for the heat of the day before he got his ropes out and began ripping down the altars. He tied four lines on each of the poles before attaching them to the very girth of the Percheron. The gigantic horse became more ferocious with every pull, the ropes cutting into his testicles as the sweat rolled from his body and soaked the Lutheran.

Billy saw six of them tumble to the ground before she was covered in dust, the head of the Percheron rearing up again and again. Within minutes hers was the only one standing, the graves closest falling with a slow torpor as the new wood refused to give under the tired haunches of the draft. But they soon became part of the rubble.

"All for Billy."

The Lutheran spoke from the vicinity of the gored brave but she couldn't see him until his body cut out of the heat and dirt to become a piece of the confusion drifting, the dirty color of chaos from his head to the Percheron's hooves. He'd taken some fresh booty and it covered his warhorse like cold black gravy, everything from the feathers of eagles to the bones of women. All the Lutheran's movements begged for an Armageddon.

From where she was tied she could smell burnt flesh and bloated carcass, the scent of the man before her, his prancing amongst the devastated holy ground as opposite to pure as death is to life. Knowing she was attentive he smiled and beat his chest, saying "all for Billy" until he was drunk with the words themselves.

He paraded for the better part of an hour before climbing up to pour water in her mouth. Billy spit it out through dry lips and the Lutheran laughed. He counted her wounds and announced the number, not turning away until he saw grass bend a mile away.

"Pigs. Wild pigs," he said.

The Lutheran hopped down and prepared his weapons as the first of the feral pigs broke into the open amongst the toppled platforms and began rooting for flesh. The animals were set low to the ground, their skin between tan and dark brown with minion builds like something from the underworld. Each of them ground their short tusks into the piles of soft wood and they found parts to eat but could not be satisfied.

Threadbare let a pack of twenty get into the clearing before he left his stead to pursue them, their squeals and grunts rising up into a crescendo of panic as he killed four with his first round of shots, the pistol and the Long Tom repetitive as if each were automatic. If they tried to escape the Percheron would overrule the kicking commands of the Lutheran and jump after them until he crushed them underfoot. Some gave challenge but these were let go as if the Lutheran expected them to tell other beasts that a new commander had been cut loose and he alone ruled the frontier.

Billy watched the face of the Lutheran, his dark eyes paralyzed in hate. She wondered if there was a place where children could be born and never see such a sight. She had no idea if her family was dead so she asked God if this Threadbare would be allowed to stay on earth for eternity but he did not answer.

"Mama! Mama!"

When Torq and Latham walked underneath her altar Billy thought the sun had taken her better sense. The boys had disobeyed their father, untying themselves where he'd secured each to the travois more than an hour's walk away.

Torq had enough of Moba's training to stay on the trail they'd been following and Latham wouldn't let him go alone. Their father was making a wide circle because he knew what would happen if he invited an ambush. He was still on the high side of the Lutheran and out of range as the children meandered onto the scene like sheep.

"Thirsty mama. I'm thirsty," said Torq.

"Back. Back boys. Back to your father. You've got to go back to daddy."

Billy whispered as they looked up thinking nothing was beyond the ordinary as a child's mind often does. It was a game to them and though the game was ugly and shots from the Lutheran were ripping up divots all around still they pursued care.

"Come down mama! Come down!" Billy tried to calm them but the excitement in their voices continued to swell.

When the Lutheran saw them he pulled away from chasing a gut shot pig and stopped dead in his tracks to turn the horse. A broad smile came across his lips and he laughed at the irony of it all, twisting to pull out the bars he used for false teeth before banging them on the cantle of his saddle and reinserting them.

"The small. The little small Mox's," he said.

The Lutheran got off his horse and went over to one of the dead pigs as the boys continued to talk to their mother. He opened up the belly of the animal with his knife and in the tradition of those crazed torn breeds, those products of violence against pilgrims, their blood as much Mexican as white and as much white as Plains Indian, he put three red streaks across his chest and then two from his eyes to his throat and there was nothing more frightening, not even in a nightmare. And he knew it would all end here.

"They've come to see the Lutheran. Billy, show them me," he said.

Jumping back in the saddle he drew out his big knife and put the Long Tom and short blade back in their scabbards. When the Lutheran spun around to close on the children Billy heard the shuffle and began screaming.

"Run boys! It's your life! Into the high grass with all you have!"

When it registered Billy could see it in the eyes of Torq, the boy grabbing his brother's hand and bolting into the waving grass just as the Lutheran reached top speed, leaning over the right side of his animal while pitching the long blade from handle to tip in his imposing hand. Galloping beneath Billy he dropped down even more to make it clean and when he did Dampier stood up directly in his path and sent a shot from the .52 caliber, a blast striking him just below the Adam's apple and sending the Lutheran flying off the back of the Percheron. When he landed he went limp and there was no rise in his blackened chest.

Dampier went over and kicked his ribcage, brandishing the reloaded pistol but there was no movement. He looked down and spoke before going to collect his children and free his wife.

"That's enough. Enough for this life and the next. Back to hell with you."

33

He lay still, the counts in his chest and the light in the eyes dimming, then coming back, a throttling pain where his voice comes from but there's no helping it because he can't move his hands. In his head he says I can't move my hands and this must be death.

There's someone standing over him inviting him to hell but he doesn't believe it because he can't think of dying. He sees the shot again in a memory going back to the killing of the pigs and a few settlers and then the fire from the man Mox's big pistol but he's not done for yet, it's not time to leave this life yet.

The children come over to look at the hole in his throat but no one touches him except the black one. Little dark Torq who'll soon kill just like him for years are nothing when you live day to day. He tries to speak to the boy but no words will come out.

Later that night a pair of women speaking Shoshonean grab him by the ankles. He understands most of what they say as they reiterate the command from the Comanche Dipping Bird who's instructed the women to pull him from the sacred site and then let the animals have the big white's body. Dipping Bird wants

Threadbare to pass through the bowels of the scavengers and then go back to dust in shame, always in shame they say, for he'll go nowhere dishonored.

As the women struggle through the grass they lose their breath. The Lutheran's head is dragging down the high foliage making it laborious so they stop, one of the women saying she saw a gunfight with a pair of ancient dueling pistols between a lawman from the Arkansas Territory and this very same man beneath them.

She says she remembers the Lutheran making a formal show and although she was a little girl she could understand their white words, the man with the badge saying the Lutheran had killed a bad man but was still to be judged. The lawman would hear of no excuse and the Lutheran didn't offer any.

The Comanche woman said they were both tough men with no fear of death so they took twenty steps backwards before shooting. The lawman fired first and wounded the Lutheran but he did not fall. As the lawman waited for the Lutheran to return the shot he waited too long, for the big white walked over to his horse and pulled out a musket, making his way over to the lawman who stood still and only moved when the Lutheran's pistol was pitched to him underhand. When he raised his arms to catch it he was blown in half at close range. She could not understand what froze the man from Arkansas but she knew evil was hypnotic.

Threadbare lost the voice of the Comanche woman and then they stopped dragging. The one who talks the most mentions something about his teeth and then opens his mouth. She says she remembers him cleaning them after killing the lawman.

When she has them out she looks each piece over and then hands one to her friend. She enters his mouth once more and runs her fingers back while pushing on the outside of his throat, pulling out the lodged pistol ball from the inside. He wants to choke but his body won't move. He wonders why death won't even look him over and then his chest fills with air and he begins to quietly breathe.

One of the women warbles with her tongue and when she does a bird answers somewhere out on the plain and then a coyote. The Lutheran thinks to himself that these are things the natives know so he lets her finish as the pounding in his chest increases with anger, his wind more and more difficult to grasp but still it comes.

He'll fix it he thinks. If not him then he'll go to the blind woman in the Antelope Hills east of the plains and she can remedy what's left. She cured his back when the lion came out of the rocks and tore him to pieces. She used the tongue of an ox and made some liniment and now it was strong though scarred. The woman knew card tricks although she could not see them. She said the Lutheran could use them on the whites pushing their cattle westward to take over the lands of the tribes.

"I've no kin and could care less for your killing ways," she'd said.

The Lutheran let the Comanche women draw in the coyotes and strip him while asking questions about his horse. They'd seen the animal but claimed that it would sit in the grass until the resurrection of the man called Threadbare and only then would it come forward. They were superstitious and smelled of the white man's alcohol although he could feel their young skin.

"Him quit bounty," said one of the women.

Her partner knew what she was saying but couldn't repeat any of the white words. Laughing, she lay over the body of the Lutheran as he rose from his back and rolled the two women into his broad and fetid arms. He held them while the scavengers crept to the edge of the burial ground looking for the fresh kill.

34

"We should get out of here before night comes Dampier."

"And go where? It's been a week and not one Indian has shown himself. The bacon we threw out was even ignored by the rodents. They ain't nothing out there Billy. We just need to go about our business. I've got most of the cattle back and they ain't no threat of prairie burn as far as I can see."

"But he ain't dead enough and the law doesn't know he's gone. You should've put a couple more in his hide to make sure."

"That's not my way. The man was plenty dead and there's no law to tell. Let the Comanche do the bidding if he survives. We saw ten on the way back who'd been mixing with Apache's and there ain't a tribe in a thousand miles that doesn't want that bastard. He's done in. You just take care of yourself. Ain't you had enough?"

"There ain't no having enough out here. You'd think me coming from the west it'd be easier. Let's get into town and see what's left."

"I'll go Billy, but you wait till Sunday. I can keep them corralled on Sunday."

"Those cows don't give a good goddamned when you put them up Dampier! They don't know the difference!"

"You ain't a cow."

She loved everything about him although he frustrated her daily. Dampier could look through all their struggles and pick out the strangest peccadilloes to launch at Billy in the most humorous ways. He'd been so soft since bringing her back from those torturous hours that she wanted to do everything right though she felt she'd failed instantly.

Billy had made love to him the night after they'd gotten back, wincing with every turn as her broken body healed. Dampier told her that even if their lives became nothing there would always be a bloom as long as he could awaken next to her. And she had cried, letting loose the tears of fending off the tragedy thrown at her and all of the deaths they'd seen. Aging beyond her years she had the feeling that something was pushing her over and she couldn't resist. Any femininity she had was now weighted with a heavy vertigo.

The boys walked out behind them to look at the fresh grave of Moba while Billy asked herself why it all came to this. Latham wanted to know why mama's wrists and ankles had to be wrapped so she and Dampier told them, beginning with the death of her parents and what Dampier had done to defend himself before he met Billy.

They understood as children do, making it more of a mystery than reality. Their parents were players in a past scene, actors stepping out of a character to be cleansed in the showers of articulate forgiveness. You couldn't hide the dry dusty tides of the lawless frontier and they made no attempt to, giving the boys such an unsterilized version of the truth that the questions came like gunfire.

"But you've only kilted that man?" Latham asked but Torq already knew the answer.

"Well Latham, I've..."

"Daddy only did it once to protect us," interrupted Billy.

A set of cirrus clouds danced above them as Billy told the lie. There was a snap in the heat signaling fall and the breeze was picking up. Something stood up tall out on the prairie. Torq said it was a monster as Latham began to cry. Billy asked him to apologize and he said no, Dampier saying nothing as Billy knocked him to the ground and the boy understood.

"I love you Dampier, but I want to see his bones," she said. "He can't come back from the dust."

35

The rains came as he crossed east on his way to the Antelope Hills. His neck bled freely and ran into the waist of his pants in a red stream as he kept his head down to protect the hole in his neck, the Lutheran bouncing on the back of the Percheron like some cancerous Lazarus visited upon the face of a new world. In his mind he was now invincible because both time and reaper had fallen before him but still he sped onward, a quintessential mockery of what humans could create.

On the fifth hour of his journey he rode into the camp of three Texans traveled too far north to rustle Mexican cattle. They were sitting around a campfire, fifty head lowing with hacienda brands creating a wall around them. When they saw him each popped up like blooming lousewort to draw their pistols, speaking out in Spanish and then English for the horseman to introduce himself but by then it was too late.

The Lutheran raised his head and shook the water from the brim of his hat, throwing it into the air as the first cowboy fired, knocking the hat from its orbit and lifting his attention just enough so he could have his throat cut at a full gallop. The other two began shooting wildly in all directions and as they spent their final powder Threadbare turned the Percheron in the dark and came back to trounce them where they stood shoulder to shoulder. The one surviving the rush began screaming out in the language of Threadbare's youth so he stalled, got off his horse and went over to pick up his hat.

The man begged to be spared, talking through bloody lips about the shores of Iceland and the Norwegian sea, telling Threadbare that there was enough room for them to run rampant over the Americans in the west if he'd only let him live.

The Lutheran watched the man as the downpour increased and searched himself for sympathy after not hearing the tongue of his homeland for so many years. He then snapped his fingers twice and the Percheron came over to his hip as the Lutheran reached down to pick up the broken rustler.

The man smiled when he grabbed his wrist, the grin soon fading to terror as the Lutheran pulled him beneath the animal and hissed between the bars of his teeth. The Percheron reared and crushed the man's chest instantly. When it pulled up to kill again he grabbed the reins and looked down.

"I'm west of Missouri. All west of Missouri. No room for you," he whispered.

36

The blind woman smelled him when he rode up to the mouth of her hovel. She called out in the language of the Sioux and he did not respond. When she tried the Caddoan of the Kiowa he gave a brief greeting, ducking into the small house built into the side of a hill to sit before her fire.

"He didn't kill you?"

"Neck," said the Lutheran with difficulty.

"Their blood will get you. They're the only ones who'll stay on the plains with no fear of the Comanche or the Apache. The sons..."

"Neck," repeated the Lutheran.

She made her way around the stark room like she had eyes and put her hands on his face, cringing with what she felt, a face too horrible to mention. The blind woman had treated every killer from the Carolina's to the Pacific but there was none more vicious than the Lutheran. He'd made holes on top of holes in all parts of his body but he never lost the lust for butchery.

"A ball?" She was feeling the hole and moving the loose tissue around and smelling the wind that came through it.

"He shot near," he replied.

"You should be dead. The wind comes through mouth and nose and the older you get the less it comes but you should be dead."

"I stand."

She felt around on the interior of his windpipe and made a few comments about the taking of his food. He said he would not eat until it was healed but that's not what she meant.

"That could be a lifetime," she said. "I'll sew it and patch it with the root of Ponder but you'll die if you don't eat."

"It comes as it comes and it came heavy with the man Mox. But I stand."

The Lutheran had put the words together out of anger. It titillated him to overpower the talk of the Americans since he'd spent so much time bringing grief to the tribes and mastering their languages.

"You scar easy Lutheran. They come up on you like a child and they stay with you like something lost."

There was a plate over her fire with rounded edges and a hole in the middle.

She went to a cabinet hanging from a timber in the ceiling and pulled out a green root that came from the same place as the weed of the sea. She began to give him a history but he snapped at her, saying he didn't care for her tales.

"The root of Ponder will do," he said. "Do your work old woman."

She started a low and haunting chant and when she did the rain opened up in the sky and began to leak through the roof but she did not stop her music. The blind woman pitched the root behind her as she ran her hands over the sweating body of the Lutheran. It landed in the middle of the plate and began smoking, filling the room with an acrid smell. The Lutheran raised his hand and brushed her away but she grabbed him by the wrist and sat him back down.

"It all comes with the root. The smoke, smell, taste and touch."

"Finish it or you're dead old woman."

"Never come this way again Lutheran. Even when the whites cover us and roll up the dead Mexicans never come this way again. You've gone beyond mad and I don't want you in my presence."

Behind her the green root began to make a liquid that ran into the hole. When it lost its humidity she went over and picked it up with the tip of her fingers as the Percheron wedged his head in the doorway, its nostrils checking on its keeper.

"Still now," she said.

The old woman showed the cluster of root to the black eyes of Threadbare and then pried his lips apart and forced a small piece into his mouth. He chewed it slowly, his face smoking like a cup of chicory coffee.

"True evil you are Threadbare."

She waited for him to swallow before jamming the dryness of the remaining root into the wound on his throat. The Lutheran bit down then reached for her before drawing back.

"Never come this way again," she said.

37

They left the boys with a Mason named Haw Plil in Reckingfort Soo, a twenty year old horse trader from Vermont who thirty years later would defect from his own state to fight for the Confederacy with the past struggle of the Texans fresh on his mind. The time and place he was shot down is etched on a stone marked CSA 51. It lies in the hills of Northwestern Alabama. He was alone the night he died. His wife Shon never made it out of Reckingfort Soo.

"Dampier, those other folks aren't staying. That leaves me and Shon."

"It'll just take a day or so Haw. If they're any trouble put the strap to them."

"With her pregnant I guess I should get some practice because there isn't any other way to raise them except rough out here."

Haw Plil had stepped out of his house and was looking up and down the street of Reckingfort Soo. His family was the only one left but he'd secured a solid niche with the Mexicans who'd heard of the big Kentucky horses and wanted them for their Cavalry. Plil had provided ten so far and had requests for five more. He was wary of the promises from the officers, though they paid in cash and had given him a few deeds to some useless tundra with no water.

"We'll be fine Dampier. How's that Billy?"

"She said goodbye to them out a ways. She's waiting on me. She's apt to believe that Lutheran..."

"No need to tell it again. I heard about it," replied Plil.

Both of the boys had gone down the street and were looking out on the plains for their mother. When Dampier called they returned and stood at the feet of Haw Plil. He looked down at them and smiled, Torq reaching out to grab him by the pants leg and twist the fabric until it went tight on his knee.

"Can I help you sir?" Haw looked into the eyes of Torq.

"Seeing if you're gunned up," said Torq.

"Learns early for such a young one."

"And uses every bit of it," replied Dampier.

Dampier leaned over and saw his wife Shon sitting at a table at the far end of the house. Haw had expanded by knocking down a wall and doubling the size of the home. She was staring into the emptiness of the new room with her hands below her huge belly singing a quiet song to the unborn.

"Shon," said Dampier.

"Pregnant and getting pregnanter if that's a word. Be sure and tell the horse trader there that as soon as the Indians or Mexicans kill us he needs to get somebody to give you the will. Oh, but there's nothing to give."

Her sarcasm fit well on the East Coast but on the plains of the frontier it was intolerable. The woman stopped singing and walked over to a cabinet, pulling out a bottle of bourbon before taking a large swill and sitting back down. Some dust fell in her hair and she began to cry.

"Are you sure this'll be okay Haw?" Dampier was concerned and wondering about the decision.

"I told her she's going to make the baby a drunk before its born but my words go unheeded. She's not much for my proposals. You think you could get Billy to come over and give her a few lessons on how to do it?"

"Do what?"

"Just accept it. The flat. The killing. The Indians. I mean we got a whole town to ourselves and that's something."

"Aw hell Haw, Billy's better at it than me and she ain't telling her secrets."

Both of the boys walked past Haw to talk to the woman Shon. Torq asked her why she was so fat and Shon pointed at her husband. Latham wanted to know about the bad smell so she raised her finger and looped it around her head.

"Every goddamn thing about this place stinks boy! Now get out!"

"No reason to talk so harsh Shon," a voice responded.

Billy had come around to a back window and was speaking through a crack in the sod next to the frame. She tapped twice as Haw came over and opened it, reaching through to grab Billy's hand and shake it enthusiastically.

"Hey, hey Miss Billy! I'm glad to see you lady! How are you?"

"Fine Haw. It's good to see you. Listen, to save words I'm telling you that

I ain't leaving my brood with this bitch if she's drinking her own to death before it's born."

"Billy," said Dampier.

"No, it's fine. We'll be fine. Won't we be fine Shon?"

"We'll do the best we can loving husband." The woman grinned at everyone in the room and then changed her expression into a fake giggle.

Billy and Dampier met each other at the front door while Shon got up and took her chair into the cool darkness of the addition to sit by herself and pout. Latham followed and tried to climb into her lap but she covered her face with both hands so he walked away. Haw watched the incident and then stepped outside.

"You'd do well to get that woman back to a city," said Billy.

"We weren't exactly from a city in Vermont. Shon just liked knowing she was born on the first side of the country and not the last."

"This son of a bitch is the last of everything," added Dampier.

"Yes it tis', but there's more," said Haw.

The three stood in the street looking behind the houses on either side at the steppes rolling for miles before them, their contours not stopping until they met the eroded peneplain of an unborn Nebraska with parts of its body resembling the surface of the moon. The woman Shon listened to them as they spoke and she found no fascination in what they saw and couldn't comprehend their need to enter where they did not belong. She'd called her husband a "displacer" when the black ice had fallen that February and told him that such a home was no home at all. Now she sat with Torq and Latham looking at her, having no other thoughts but to return to civilization, the children at her feet living in the only one they knew.

"Take your time. I'll handle this. Do what you need to." Haw raised his hand to them as they walked to their wagon.

"We won't and you must," replied Billy.

The Lutheran wouldn't be found where they were going because he rode north of them crossing the east west running Canadian like a mother braiding hair. He looked at the prints of animals on the muddy banks, saying their names in English before stopping and stripping off his clothes to bathe.

While he was in the warm water a storm blew up twenty miles northeast. He watched the rain fall like white Paiute lances in its center, a tornado coming out and twisting on an ocean of plain and then it was gone. The wind from it caught him in the back as he dressed and there was a deer he could see but it was too far to shoot.

When he unsaddled the Percheron the animal walked into the water, the bank rising where it entered. The horse took several big gulps and then went to the middle but still it was not under past the withers. The Lutheran hissed and the beast turned its head. He made some gesture with his hand and it spun a quarter turn more so he could see.

Tied to the horse was a black and gray mass floating on the river's surface the Lutheran didn't want wet. Small fish were coming up to nibble on its greasy texture as a vulture sat down on the opposite bank clicking its lazy claws. The Lutheran shook his head and waded out to the Percheron. He untied a loop of rope around the animal's neck and brought the bundle from the water, squeezing out the excess before snapping it, the droplets flying from the scalp of the blind woman as the buzzard lifted into the air making a repulsive shadow. He put the scalp on the bank and it began to dry in the post-storm calm.

38

They came up on Plimpton three hours from the burial ground. He was leaning against a piece of volcanic rock mashing up bread in the bottom of a tin plate before a small fire. He had a flask filled with goat's milk and was pouring it on the crusty bread while looking around for his shirt as Billy and Dampier approached. They could see his ample gut from ten minutes out, a musket perched on the fat. Plimpton was repeating the movement of pointing the weapon and drawing it away, taking a little bite of mash before looking again.

"If he does it one more time I'm taking a shot," said Dampier.

"You hot for the kill my darling?" Billy looked over at Dampier as they stopped, still not speaking to Plimpton who had the musket leveled but wouldn't talk while chewing.

"Sir, don't do that!" Billy yelled at him and he lifted his double chin to have a look.

"Are you two meanin to kill me? Cause if you are I aim to do the killin first!"

"Do we look like killers?" Dampier put both hands up and when he did the man turned the barrel of the musket and fired into the emptiness above their heads.

"Whoa now! Whoa a damn minute!" Dampier called out but didn't wait for the response. He pulled up his own and sent a ball careening off the rock next to the man's head as Billy jumped from the wagon and began stomping over to where Plimpton sat prepping the musket for another shot. She caught him underneath the chin with the toe of her boot just as he plugged the powder horn with his left hand, the cork coming out as the black granules flew into his eyes and Plimpton fell on his side.

"A goddamned trader Dampier! He's a murderous goddamned slaver out here poking for Comanche women for the brothels! I hope you enjoy being by yourself because I'm going to burn you in one lump just like the Comanche would if they caught you hunting their women! You hear me fat man!"

Billy was incensed at Plimpton's behavior. More so since she could guess his profession from what sat around him. There were small vials filled with Laudanum and smoky bottles of pure alcohol with a syringe and some liquid she could not see. He had a bag of handcuffs made from waxed rope and a set of maps as detailed as one could find for the Mexican Province. He was on his way back to New Orleans and had made camp after sighting the two Comanche women sent to remove Threadbare several days before. He'd been waiting but they were long since dead.

"What are you, a scout?"

Dampier had come up while the man was spitting out his two front teeth. Plimpton wouldn't answer but they both knew others were in the area carrying the tiny cages holding the women until they got to the port city, many used up or dying en route before they arrived.

Billy rolled a cigarette while she thought about the low end results of God creating humans like this. She took a draw and handed it to Dampier who had a pull and then gave it back. When she flicked it on the man the powder lit on his face and shoulder in a blue flash but they put him out before any permanent damage was done.

"No more! No more," he said.

"What've you seen?" Dampier asked him inquisitively after breaking his musket over the rock and peppering a little more powder on the groin of Plimpton's pants.

"I ain't seen a goddamned thing you pioneer, red lovin son of a bitch!"

"That ain't gonna do," said Billy. She picked up the cigarette and put it between her thumb and index finger just as Dampier grabbed her hand.

"Have you been up to the burial grounds," asked Dampier.

"Hell yes! I passed right through there. I run across these two squaws walkin out that way. I came right through 'em but lost the track. They gotta come this way though, their people are movin south of the Soo."

"Did you see a man neck shot? Had the birds got on a big man with white hair when you..."

"Billy, he may have come through before all that."

"No he didn't! He's been there since and had to come across him!"

"They ain't no such thing there," Plimpton said. "I know what you're lookin for though. We all know about him."

"What did you see," Billy asked.

"Just the regular. A bunch of dead Comanche's and some tear up. I don't know the place though, I ain't from here 'bouts."

Billy bent to burn him but Dampier stopped her. She looked from her husband's hand up to his face where the answer was obvious though he wouldn't admit it without proof.

"God means to punish us," she said.

Dampier refused to believe the man so they pushed on, passing the consorts of the flesh dealer before the day was out. As the wheels of their wagon bumped and creaked over the uneven surface they came upon three men on horseback, another riding what looked to be a death cart, its construction harried from the floors of sawmills north of New Orleans. Stacked three high in the back of the wagon were the rectangular cages used to travel country slaves from Spanish Florida to the upper reaches of the Chesapeake. On the bottom of the stack Billy could see the fingers of a young woman and hear her cries in a language not spoken in the ranges near Reckingfort Soo.

When they were abreast of the slavers the one on the wagon began speaking to Dampier in French, making lewd comments towards Billy while darting his tongue in and out of his mouth through a filthy red beard. Their tactic was ancient and they expected Dampier's wife to be easily taken.

Expecting a fight Dampier reached between his legs as the other horsemen circled but it was too late. Billy was one step ahead of him, the .52 caliber having already been leveled at the ribald merchant, his eyes widening as she pulled back the hammer and spoke in a slow drawl.

"You tell them to come back around or you'll have a hole in your head. You know what I'm saying."

The men on horseback all understood. They made their way back in line as the wagoneer raised his hands in the air. Billy began to jump off and make a stand for the girl but as she did Dampier reached across and put his arm around her.

"No Billy. There's too many. Another day. They'll kill us four on two."

She let it go, both she and Dampier turning in their seat, their weapons on the men as they rode away. Billy didn't put the .52 caliber up until they were spots on the plain, keeping her back to her husband the entire time. When they arrived at the burial ground they found what Billy feared most.

39

Plimpton saw the four Frenchmen and broke his camp. They didn't ask about his burns or if he'd found any other women to sell. There were no words exchanged about Billy or Dampier, the problem of the couple not being something that concerned them or their mission.

As Plimpton crawled in the back of the wagon they made jokes about his girth, gesticulating in bastardized French about the wagon tilting backwards as he raped the young woman after dragging her from the cage and unbuckling his pants. There was a short stop so they could all do the same and then they moved on.

That night the men camped apart on the North Fork of the Red River when they should've shared a fire, their mistake not being their profession as it had been with a violently precocious Billy and a well armed Dampier. It all became a question of position, for on that Fall night in the year 1831 the slavers from New Orleans unknowingly placed themselves due south of a slow running Canadian, their bold wagon tracks bringing the Lutheran to their camp in an easy lope. He drowned them all individually in that creeping fork of the Red, none of them knowing their counterparts were dead until he told the fat man that there would be no morning. Plimpton gave no response.

While setting fire to the wagon he heard the female scream from the lowest compartment. He backed around to make sure her cage was locked before pulling the Percheron's head toward Reckingfort Soo, all having been held responsible in the wake of the Lutheran.

40

Shon Plil was drunk when Haw asked her if she thought it would be better if he didn't go. They were standing in the kitchen of their house, having no idea that Billy and Dampier had turned at the burial site after seeing the place empty, the wreckage of the bones still present. They had broken an axle on the way back and were on foot, so far out on the plain they could do nothing to stop what would happen.

"Shon, if you can't handle the boys by yourself I'll stay."

"Go on Haw! I'm fine, they do a good job of entertaining themselves."

Shon was swaying from side to side in front of him threatening to fall.

"I wish you'd come off the bottle a little. It can't be good for the baby."

"I'll come off when you get me away from these flats and back to the mountains," she said.

He hesitated, "I won't be more than a half day. Captain Verraco says that last thoroughbred had a split hoof but it doesn't. He'll make trouble, but I'll get out of it. If he's shot the horse I'm in a hell of a fix."

"Shoot the Mexican bastard! I hate those people!"

"Shon, I can't shoot the people I supply. Maybe I'll swing by and see if Dipping Bird has any interest if the Mexicans won't trade anymore."

"Let's just leave. The Indians will kill you..."

"Please Shon, go a little easy. There's money to be made out here and it doesn't help with you complaining."

"I'll pray for you," she said contemptuously.

He leaned over to kiss her and she turned away, walking over to shut the window before making her way to the bed. He let the slight go as he'd done for many months, his wife still ill adapted to a forced life on the plains.

Haw Plil went outside and saw Torq and Latham piling up stacks of forgotten furniture next to his gelding. They'd managed to make a large enough heap to put the saddle on but neither of them could lift it past their chests.

"What are you two together, six years old?"

"Free and free," slurred Torq.

"You're not three and neither is he," joked Haw.

Torq looked up with his black eyes and then across at Latham who was looking at the ground. He was thinking of something to say but couldn't put it together after so much intensive labor came to nothing.

"You guys would be deadly on each other's shoulders. But it's best not to rob people who aren't here. They might come back for you."

"Torq done it," said Latham. "Me no help."

Haw saddled the horse and let each take a turn on the gelding, neither having any fear of the swatting tail or the height of its back. While pulling Torq from the animal he saw the mark.

"Big white with click click teeth made word. It say LOST. No come off."

Torq made the face of the man that had branded him but Haw didn't laugh. There was something in the boy seen in men who carried bullets in their chests or had been kicked by horses. If they lived they were either damned with slowness or uplifted with a morbid instinct as if they knew something you didn't. They had a preference for heat instead of cold but their souls were the latter.

"You boys know how to get into the cellar if a big blow comes? And how to get to the food if Shon is asleep or not feeling good?"

Torq held his finger up and answered for both of them. Latham became even more withdrawn knowing he'd be left with his brother and the drunken woman with the big belly.

"I'll be back soon," Haw said.

When he turned the mount west Torq blew out between his teeth and said goodbye to him in Shoshonean. When the horse heard it he spun around to throw Haw but the man spurred outwards and pushed in his toes.

"Learn a little Comanche out there with your daddy Torq?"

"Coo-manch," replied the boy.

Both watched him make his way out of town before the wind changed its direction, switching ninety degrees from the east with a chilly blast that lifted the hat off the head of Haw Plil and sent him running across the prairie. After he caught it he looked back at Reckingfort Soo and saw the dust rise up in the streets but the boys hadn't moved. Latham was covering his eyes and Shon had come to the door to shut it. He thought he heard her call out to them but she hadn't.

Torq walked to the end of the street teetering with every gust as Latham went over to the front door of the Plil house and knocked, sitting down on the stoop like a dog when the woman wouldn't let him in. He began crying after several minutes when the wind refused to calm, balling up with his head in his lap to hide from the world.

"You go play," screamed the woman Shon. He remained where he was.

Torq stayed in the streets until the sun set and an orange glow covered the plain. He was anonymous to everything about him, thinking he must be the only boy on earth. How big it was he thought, all colors brown or those more feeble shades that dance around red. They lit up his dark eyes and stoic features and he wished his father was there but he wasn't, for the man Dampier was running slowly across the plain towards Reckingfort Soo, Billy saying she couldn't go on but he must for the man would be coming and her twisted ankle would only slow them. She said she'd seen worse than a long hobble across the plain and it didn't scare her.

"He's coming Dampier. They ain't no dead in him."

When Torq saw the prairie dog scramble he was still within earshot of Shon. By the time he followed it onto the expanse the town was gone and the dark was upon him. He thought he heard his brother banging on the door of the house but Latham would be out there till morning.

Torq lost his direction and couldn't get back so when he heard the horse he screamed. When it went into a gallop he got down on his stomach to play the game of the Comanche, listening to see how close the animal was as it closed, the ground sending back thunder and getting dirt in his eyes as honest tears began to fall.

When he was ripped from the floor of the plains and brought up into the saddle he began to cry like any lost boy.

"Home that way," he said. But there was no answer.

Running Color

The cat had its face up to the window. A beam of sunlight bathed the feline as it reached out to grab it with a paw, lounging on the jailhouse floor beneath a calendar reading August 1, 1844.

Behind the cat in a single cell was a fourteen year old who'd taken the bread he was given and after putting his large hands through the bar dropped it to entice the cat. He pulled its attention away by making shapes with his hands from his own shaft of light, a fluttering Yellowhammer and then a Pheasant. The animal couldn't decide between bread or meat.

"Little kitty cat, ssss, get it, get the pretty bird."

He brought the animal through the bars when it turned to the bread, walking over and sitting on the floor to pick fleas from its back, pushing it through his iron striped window when the front door opened.

"Where's that goddamned cat?"

The man came in but the boy didn't notice him. With his hands up the Sheriff could see his wide back and broad shoulders, his body a mixture of field hand and blacksmith even at a young age.

"Hey little lost boy, your mother sent you another envelope full of cash. You want me to keep it for you. You ain't gonna need it after the hanging. How does she know where you are anyway?"

"*Se rumorea que es una puta por las vacas,*" said the young man.

"I know you called me a whore! Or a cow poker! You speak American you lil' bastard! We're an independent republic since '36 and there's talk of us being admitted to the Union. Damn shame you had to shoot up three Texans along with the others. Otherwise you'd be free to roam."

"Killing is killing," said the young man.

"Not when you walk into a saloon in Rio Bravo and just open up on the first American that asks you why you're there. There were troops of both colors in that town so you killed a few of both."

"They shouldn't have taken time for booze and lust. Especially together."

"They shouldn't of ever cut the iron for the Colt Paterson as far as you're concerned," the Sheriff answered.

"I like five shots. When I started killing I only got one."

"When was that?" The Sheriff became interested with the flow of information so he walked over to the cell with the kid's very own gun to wait for the answer.

"Knifed a Chippewa and a Cree while they were fishing on the Missouri." The kid began to move around the cell so the Sheriff stepped back.

"How long ago," asked the Sheriff.

"Five years. You do the figuring."

"What'd they do?"

"They were fishing stupid," the kid said.

"That don't seem like no reason to kill a man."

"I'd kill you for less you stinking son of a bitch."

"You ain't gonna get the chance."

"Wanna go fish," said the kid.

The Sheriff left him alone to read the letter his mother had sent. All the money had been taken out and her script ripped in half. In it she said his father had sold five hundred head to an American and that people were beginning to move back to Reckingfort Soo. They'd bought all the land between the homestead and the town and had even gotten legal deeds with the Texans.

The letter had passed through several posts and had finally found him as a result of his capture. She wouldn't know about the hanging yet, that being best, because if she did his brother would be on the way and that'd just fill another grave.

"He wouldn't make it past the first river," the boy said.

Torq dropped the letter to his waist and looked out at the Rio Grande in the distance. The small town of Infidente was on the other side, the river still four years from becoming the official southern border of a growing Texas. There was nothing but desert around him and he thought it a cruel joke to store your criminals in such conditions before you took them down river to kill them. He knew of twenty different men that'd been through there and not one had come out alive.

"You've got to go to the river," he said to himself.

"You're too young to swim it." The voice came from Torq's back and he turned to see a priest holding the cat in his arms, the animal's eyes once again locked on the shaft of light as it crawled across the floor and the day brightened.

"You here to bring me salvation Father Epigo?"

"Until they hang you Torq Mox. Which it looks like they'll successfully do this time."

"You ain't told her my whereabouts have you? Did you go through the Soo?"

"I saw her and your dad two months ago. She said she sent a letter to Austin but with Texas independent she didn't think it'd get to you."

"I got it. Does she..."

"No, she doesn't know about your blood lust. She thinks you live a quiet life somewhere empty and don't want to be bothered. But it's been over a decade Torq."

"They should've kept a closer eye on me and that time wouldn't have been filled up with powder burns and harlots. I ain't got nothing against them, but I ain't got no need to visit. Does she still take the money from the old man when he ain't looking and then lie about it."

"Torq, you're just a boy. Still a boy," the priest said.

"With thirteen I've put in coffins padre. If daddy knew I was alive then it wouldn't be as fun. But goddamn Father Epigo, they got enough cash to do them for a century so why not make sure Latham don't sour?"

"You'll pay for the innocents Torq."

"You'll pay for taking that collar off to go into *los burdeles*. Or does it hurt less when I call them whorehouses padre? Either way you're defrocked and willing as I. To hell with you."

Father Epigo didn't answer and didn't like being so far from home. The priest had met Billy and Dampier as a citizen of Mexico six months after Torq was taken. He'd learned English in the independent republic of Fredonia before it failed and was summarily tossed from his diocese by a direct order from Mexico City. He refused to take off his collar for reasons of safety and belief.

Epigo hunted for his living and also played a good hand of cards. When he wasn't praying with the pilgrims of Reckingfort Soo or in the heart of the Indian nations he kept Billy informed of whatever lie he could make up about her oldest son. He knew she could read him and that his tales were all but empty, but they both protected Dampier. As far as he was concerned Torq had been eaten on the prairie, and after months on end searching for the boy so long ago, him being eaten is what he chose to believe.

"How do you do it Epigo?" Torq was watching him and continuing to pick at his calm.

"*Que'*?"

"Keep the little secret from daddy. You and Billy must be tight."

"He needs it. He'll hear about your real death in less than a month so why not give him some comfort?"

"You'll never know all of it because I'll never tell."

"Those years are yours and the secrets your own," said Father Epigo.

The priest walked over to look down at Torq. The boy met him at the bars as he pulled a small glass container of Holy Water from his front pocket and dipped his finger in it. Torq leaned over and pressed his face against the bars, sticking his tongue out and applying pressure, his long dirty hair falling in front of his ears and over the hands of the priest.

"Bless away," he said. "It don't count anyway."

"Any blessing from anybody will do you good Torq. And I still believe there's good in you."

Torq's black eyes looked up at the priest, the sockets an abyss a thousand times deeper than space.

"Careful Father Epigo, my hands are still free."

42

"Now Torq, this'n don't speak nothin but Mexican so don't make plans with him and think I won't hear. He'll sleep off his drunk and then I'll take him back across."

"Chain that bastard up outside. If I wanted somebody to foul up the place I'd ask you," Torq responded.

The Sheriff drug in an inebriated man of twenty who'd fired his weapon across the river thinking the rocks on the other side were grizzlies. He was in his second day of mescal hallucinations and would've been left alone if the last ricocheting bullet wouldn't have gone through the jail's outhouse.

"*La puerta y la ventana, estan cerrada?*" The man asked the Sheriff and the Sheriff looked at Torq who let him flounder for a second.

"He wants to know if the door and window are closed," said Torq.

"Can't he see?" The Sheriff held the man's chin up to the open window and then over to the closed door.

"*Mira,*" added Torq.

"*No hay oso gris?*" The man was terrified and needed reassuring.

"No," replied Torq from the darkness.

The Sheriff handcuffed the man to a big wooden desk and sat him on the floor. His shoulders swayed for a moment and then he was out cold, snoring and talking to someone who wasn't there.

After the Sheriff had gone Torq chipped a few pieces of plaster from the cell wall with his fingernail. He wanted to get a look at the man's face because it was familiar. Father Epigo's visit had opened a vault of memory for Torq, the good and the bad coming back like offset seasons of the year.

"*Borracho!*"

The drunk looked up. When he did Torq flicked a piece of plaster between his eyes to briefly sober him.

"Atajo, you ridiculous bastard," Torq said.

"Me no know you," said Atajo.

"But I know you know what I'm saying because we're all grown up now!"

The drunk looked at Torq and then got to his feet, leaning against the weight of the desk to right himself. When Torq stepped into the light from the window the drunk screamed and began yanking at the bolted desk until his wrist broke though he refused to stop pulling.

"Atajo! Sit down before you kill yourself! I'm behind here! Look, there's bars!" Torq wrapped his fingers around them and leaned back to show how sturdy they were.

"*Y la espalda,*" said Atajo.

"You have to see it?"

"*Por favor,*" said the Mexican.

Torq pulled his hair to the back of his ears, spitting out a strand sticking to his lips before letting his shirt drop to the floor.

"*Hace frio,*" he said. The man gave no response but Torq wouldn't turn until he did.

"Cold, yes cold in night desert," replied Atajo.

"Not that cold," answered Torq.

When he spun around the man Atajo stepped towards him until the pain of the break took his breath and then he just fell. Torq spoke with his face looking into the cell.

"The Sheriff thinks it's funny Atajo. Thinks it's hilarious to call me the little lost boy. I don't need to hear that kind of talk knowing I could get angry. Being so young with that kind of pressure a boy might boil. I know you see different. You do see different, don't you?"

"Yes, I see," replied Atajo.

"Uh huh, it's been eight years but you are who you are," said Torq.

"You not killed?" The Mexican was scratching his boot heel on the floor as if he could escape through the boarding.

"Oh no *mi amigo*. I'm very alive and the wiser for it."

The Lutheran forced the child to ride the range with him until he turned five. In that time Torq witnessed every atrocity and crime known to man, running away as often as he could until the Lutheran killed a Crow on the Canadian border and took his pony. Torq was then lashed to the animal during the day and drug off at night, never seeing the Lutheran's eyes close and never speaking a word of his native tongue unless they were in a whiskey house card game or amongst women of sport, which the Lutheran never took as often as he robbed and killed their johns.

During the winter of '34 they found themselves on the Great Plains amongst the Arapaho in weather so bad the people of that nation left their camp on the Platte. Traveling south they came up on the boy and Threadbare making their way across the drifts hunting for any game that might stick its head over a rise.

While the Lutheran was speaking to their leader a warrior saw a hide pack shake. Overstepping his bounds he went over to the dead Crow's pony and untied the packs' leather thong. Torq's snowcapped head peeked from underneath to scream at the man bringing gunfire from the Lutheran. The warrior fell instantly, shot through the heart but no harm would come if the Lutheran would deal.

In exchange for passing unharmed though the territory of the Arapaho Threadbare could leave the boy or pay for the price of the warrior with his life. Never having faced such odds and assured he could take the child at a later time he reached over and cut the pack loose and the boy was taken without another word.

Torq remembered southern pushes after that, changing hands so many times that when he was unloaded at a labor camp in modern day New Mexico his mind was so full of the ether of confusion that the Creole who bought him had to speak Spanish and then Shoshonean to get a response. Torq Mox's young life had been decided over a roll of the dice in a Mexican comedor. That life was worth a plate of beans and a case of bad whiskey. The winner didn't even want him so the Creole got a deal.

The first time Torq met Atajo was amongst ten other boys from the labor camp. They were painting rocks to mark the winding trail for the Mexican military traveling north into the province bordering the Americans. Though only in his sixth year Torq had no fear of the other slaves, going amongst them to fight even when he wasn't provoked, standing off boys twice his age by threatening to kill them when they slept. By this time he was already sneaking from camp to sleep alone and gather his own food even though he was watched by the bosses who carried bone tipped whips to make examples of the unruly. Young Torq didn't want to escape until he was completely hardened.

Torq cursed them when they made fun of his mark and it was just such an occasion that Atajo recalled. The boy's name was Victor and he was the son of a prostitute from some frontier camp and he was white like Torq. He'd been handed off to every charity and a few jails until he looked upon the beginning of his adult life with a sack of rocks to paint and a kid with LOST tattooed on his back refusing to speak to him in the only thing they shared, the English language.

Finally Torq spoke up and told Victor he'd better learn the tongue of the bosses or he'd have his throat cut because they didn't like to repeat themselves and they hated any semblance of things American. Victor looked down at him and called him a motherless pig and said he'd kill him for being wise if he ever went to sleep. Torq said okay in his little boy voice and then went off when the sun sank low. The last thing he said was that Victor shouldn't pick at the youngest just because he was small.

Atajo was asleep beside Victor when Torq crawled on top of him with the arrowhead. He said something to the big American in a language Atajo didn't understand, then he cut out the boys tongue, Victor so stunned by the action he didn't even raise his hands to stop him. Torq had gone back into hiding before the pain even hit.

The next day the boss found Victor sitting by the fire, his shirt and face covered with blood. When asked who'd done this the boys all said "Apache" before little lost Torq took one step forward and threw the tongue at the boss's feet. By the next time Atajo saw him Torq Mox had learned to waste souls with an adoration given only to the depraved.

43

Latham Mox kept his collar up because the blisters on his neck hurt, three of them along a thin strip not protected from the sun on the side of his neck. He'd lost his kerchief in a rainstorm the night before and had been in the saddle since with little else to do. His father had chosen to sell out half their herd and most of the horses to invest in the railroad still seven years from making its way into a sovereign Texas. That was the time to get in he said, Dampier's nose for money was not to be protested.

The cattle that remained had been spooked over the last few days though he saw no track of animal or Indian. They grazed so close to the homestead that Billy was able to watch them from her window as they gnawed down the high grass. The drought hadn't come and the forage was plentiful, the animals staying in a tight pack for hours at a stretch.

There was branding Dampier had ordered before leaving to meet the railroad people but it totaled no more than twenty head. When Latham and Billy finished it she told him he could ride north of the river, but he best stay clear of the Comanche grasslands.

Latham passed the Coldwater and went into the flats of the Rita Blanca where he saw several Mexican vaqueros dressed in the garb of southerly gauchos, their short escopetas from a hundred years prior stuffed in the long ties around their waists. They sat astraddle hungry looking ponies and among their group were several with the high cheekbones and tight eyes more akin to the Kiowa than the eastern tribes his brother told him about in letters.

He spoke to the men in English and they just stared. When he gave a greeting in Spanish they did the same, the men not looking after him as he left, their time spent waiting silently on the prairie seemingly without cattle to tend or purpose to fulfill.

As Latham rode away several shots were fired from their stand. He guessed there must've been some treachery amongst the group but he didn't turn his horse to inquire. For a moment he scanned their faces in his mind to guess the guilty, and then he let it go.

Latham didn't feel the blisters on his neck until he'd built a fire and cooked a rabbit and by that time it was too late to do anything, his kerchief had been pushed down and he was burned. The rain began to fall and the wind picked up so he got in his saddle and turned east against it, the lightning hitting the prairie, the boys only chance to wander being protested by a God he wanted to believe in, but one that was responsible for creating a brother whose exploits were so wicked they had to be covered up by a backslidden priest and a mother on the edge of losing all control with every false update. Father Epigo hadn't ever fooled him and he knew the same was true of his mother. Torq Mox had a style that shaped his brutality and Latham thought his parents must be dense not to have figured it all out like himself.

He stayed in the saddle until he realized he was going in circles and then he just stopped. His body was uncomfortable and tired and he wanted coffee but there was no Billy to bring it.

Latham leaned forward and fell asleep, the mare beneath him grazing casually. As she ate the lullaby of the creaking saddle leather was enough to put him under before another came to him.

The visitor rode to the edge of the escarpment, the only rise of its kind in that part of the country, from there seeing Latham asleep in his saddle, thinking he was a lost pack animal or a wild horse. He brought out an expensive spyglass the French used for birding, one dueled for on a beach in Georgia. He saw clearly that the young man was sound asleep in the heat and that the rain was moving on.

"A mistake," he said to himself.

The boy's face was sweating in the lens of the glass some two miles distant. When he had him locked in sight Latham's mare perked up her ears but the boy did not move. He thought he was alone on the plain and the horse was ignored.

Instead of riding over the steep slope the man backed his animal around and made his way down the other side, deciding to kill the boy in the spyglass for no other reason than he stuck out. He pulled a .44 caliber revolver from a holster on his horse and looked it over. Just shy of five pounds the piece was made from the iron of cannon and had been bought off a former politician three years before it was seen on the mounts of the Rangers. There was no pistol more powerful in the hands of man and today it would get its test.

Before pursuing the sleeping boy he got off his horse, the step for him a short one since his legs almost touched the ground while mounted. Once the bridle, bit and heavily oiled reins were removed he pulled the saddle and blanket off and watched the heat rise from the broad back of the beast in the shade of the late afternoon. He removed his hat and pulled out a lash from his bound hair, his face covering with the thick nasty locks of a white tangle. He pulled on a few of the matted strands and the hairs came loose, filling up his palm like a shedding canine.

As he waited for the sun to drop he brought out a series of grease paints taken from the Pawnee. He smudged black, red and high yellow stripes in succession on the horse's body until it was covered nostrils to tail, lastly circling the eyes with a mixture of all three.

The man bent back his aging body, slowly turning his neck around in the socket of his shoulders until he filled with adrenaline and the fight came over him. And still the innocent slept like the saved.

He left all his tack drying on the ground and remounted the equine bare. The animal shook at the offense of the raw assault and of the heels in his sides as the man opened the horse into a full run, beating the animal on the croup with forceful strikes from the grip of the .44 before pulling it across his chest and laying back the hammer. The distance peeled away quickly.

When he was five hundred feet out he let loose a war cry but the other's horse would not awaken its rider. It could only stand there with its ears up, a hostile breeze and a practiced murderer bearing down within seconds of striking.

If Latham would've turned he could've seen the man's pupils dilate but he didn't, oblivious to the screaming and pounding until the threat was at his back pressing the muzzle against his head in a quick pass more a blur and it was then that Latham awoke, falling to the ground with the jolt of the nightmare, nothing on the plain except for his cud chewing horse and the quiet hot day.

Latham Mox never slept in the saddle again. And he never noticed his knife had been taken until he got home. Billy reassured him he'd dropped it on the plain, but even she was unsure.

"Maybe it's in the rabbit's skin," he said.

"Always check your dead," Billy responded.

44

Torq let them have their fun until six hours before the hanging. By then the people had donated their efforts to erect a new gallows so they wouldn't have to waste time carting him downriver. He could see it from the window of his cell, watching while workers built the crossbeams and drove nails into the platform. Everyone knew of his crimes and none wanted to see him grow to manhood.

In the past many had come to the lonely little jail where Torq was being held, their lynch mobs seeking vengeance for any locals harmed by the rogues passing through the little copse of dwellings on the Rio Grande. Outlaws came daily to the crossing near Infidente, some of the most feared springing their horses from its green flow. Seven of these criminals had been lynched by the inhabitants of the

102 || The Lutheran

small town.

But it was different with the killer Torq Mox, for several thought he had money in banks back east and houses the size of feudal lords he could run to if the law was on his tail. Yet he was the one who'd created the stories and instead of being the eighth man to be drug from the jail by angry citizens, the fascination and the myth bought him a few precious hours.

No one in the area really knew how old he was but his resume preceded him, and that was all the seasoning he needed to be larger than life. The boy was mythical, but still had to swing.

"That's right! You sons of bitches better light up the torches to make sure you don't miss one hammer shot or it'll break and I'll be on ya! Then your chickens and wives after that!"

It was the midnight before the dawn hanging and Torq was spending it yelling at the men putting last touches on the new gallows. The Mexican Atajo had been let out when he urinated in his pants. Atajo circled the jail after the Sheriff drug him outside and Torq waited in the dark until he saw him coming around, holding his broken wrist but wanting one last look at *El Diablo Cruz*.

When he came up to the building Torq saw him get on the tips of his toes before he reached through the cell's window and bashed Atajo's head against the bars, pulling him inward and then letting go of his hair.

"Never take a second look into hell or the door might shut behind you Atajo," said Torq.

The man went away in a dazed stumble and never came out of the river.

"I'm heavier than that Tempada! I see you out there in the dark! You'll cross the river for a goddamn white woman but you won't cross it for your own kids! *Estas escuchando tonto!*"

As Torq berated every familiar he could find someone left the light of the torches to go and get the Sheriff. As they made their way out into the desert Torq raised his voice an octave, turning his attention to the heavens with a string of expletives so offensive the religious in the group crossed themselves and he knew he'd gotten to the bone.

"You're all marked for killing! Every last one!"

With those last words he came out of the porthole and made his way over to the front corner of the cell to wait for the Sheriff. He sat down with his feet out, slamming his head against the wall till it bloodied, then slobbering all over his shirt. When he felt the dizziness he let his head fall over. The only thing visible from the door were the bottoms of his shoes and an ominous shadow. Torq was slumped over but still breathing; everything else was in limbo, catatonic but flexible, a state of comatose fire.

"Stop the hasslin right now or you'll meet the maker early! I've had enough of you Torq!"

The Sheriff could be heard coming in the front door. When he unlocked it he looked around for the night watchman but the man was nowhere to be found. He lit a lantern and began searching for answers, going over to his desk to pull open a drawer, wanting to know why the itinerary had been sacrificed instead of checking on Torq. There on a sheet of white paper was the date and column listing the men who acted as deputy's on his night off. He turned around to look at the calendar, wasting precious time.

"Goddamn Blane! Torq Mox! Has Blane been in here tonight! The night before a hangin and the bastard don't show up! I shoulda never taken it off! This is all I need! If some paper gets a holt of this we'll have us a cattle crossin of reprobates this side of the big river!"

He didn't notice that Torq wasn't standing until there was no answer and even then he still fumbled with the calendar and schedule to make sure. He was licking his mustache and counting on his fingers when he stopped and froze, seeing the end of Torq's feet sticking out from the darkness of the cell.

"You ain't asleep!"

There was no response so he turned up the flame to knock out the shadow before going over to have a look.

"Torq!"

The boy lay still.

"If you're kilt that's fine, but if you're foolin and I have to come in there it ain't gonna be fun."

He waited, then stuck the key in the figure eight lock before hesitating against his better judgment. He could see the spittle and the blood and could smell the faint scent of urine but he gave that over to Atajo. The Sheriff looked up in the top of the cell but there were no rafters for the outlaw to have hung himself.

"He's bashed in his goddamn pumpkin. I didn't think it were possible. Thought you'd go out before you died."

He opened the lock and slid the bolt. There was talking outside. The Sheriff looked out the window but no one was there. Torq still didn't move.

"Damn I wanted to hang this boy."

He stepped inside and stood over an illuminated Torq. A cold wind blew as he positioned his sidearm to defend himself but the gun stayed holstered. If you had to squat over a man it was best to keep it drawn and ready to fire. But there were certain men you never squatted over unless you could see the ground through their chests. He should've had it out and against the boy's head. See to your regret Sheriff. You're in with the lion.

"You done yourself outright dead you lil' hellbound sumbitch."

The Sheriff got back on his heels while getting down to check the pulse. When he did it was his last mistake, losing his center of gravity and that was his only chance.

"Bad move," said Torq.

The boys black eyes popped open and the sockets of the Sheriff's sunk in, a sickness coming over his face as Torq brought one leg back before snapping it in his ribcage and sending the man to the other side of the cell. Before he hit the shark fin tooth of his own gun was against his head with the hammer about to fall.

"Last words lawman," asked Torq.

"I'll save you a place next to Lucifer," the Sheriff replied.

"He came by while you were out and left me in charge. But be proud Sheriff, you're the closest anybody ever came. Adios."

He didn't even muffle the shot, finishing the Sheriff before he walked out to his very own gallows and topped them, climbing the thirteen steps and chasing away all the workers when he did. Torq Mox stood atop the new lumber looking northwest onto a desert that met the plains, those running to the end of time itself. He had a feeling there was something more sinister than himself out there and that it was coming. Prime your best Torq Mox for the unimaginable closes, his very aftermath you cannot fathom and it is that which draws you in.

45

He watched Billy and Dampier on their walk before Dampier left to go give his money to the railroad people. They were still young and though his eyes were older now he could see the sturdiness in Billy and the infectious inferiority of Dampier. The Lutheran was amazed that the man had once been a fringe outlaw of mild reputation.

As they held hands and waved their arms the hate began to rise in his chest. He could hear them making some plan free of pitfalls, free of him, even though he'd taken one of their sons and bent him early, making sure he'd become one of the most notorious the territories had seen. Torq Mox was a gun fighter and killer that'd figured the logic of that trade while his brother Latham had been reared as soft as a feather pillow. And what child is not his raising.

"Latham's nothing," the Lutheran said. "A saddle sleeper."

Billy and Dampier came within thirty feet of him in the high summer grass but they didn't look for tracks anymore. Not with the security of the coming state and the common trades with the tribes keeping both parties happy as long as a fair shake was extended.

As they passed they made mention of the son Latham and the better attributes the two had given him, Billy saying she was glad he had his daddy's height while Dampier gave the nod to the mother's sense.

"If that Torq was with us he'd be quite a contrast to his brother," said Dampier.

"Not a runt though. None of my people were runts," she responded.

"I didn't mean it like that. Torq was the oldest, Latham would be the runt."

"I know what a runt is Dampier."

The Lutheran lay in the grass listening, realizing that Dampier was either ignorant or full of so much denial he was numb to the news of the young killer. The boy's name was his name, "the brutality of T. Mox" the papers said. And if the news hadn't spread to Reckingfort Soo then the place should be destroyed.

Torq's face was everywhere east of San Jacinto and the stories of his exploits, both true and false, equaled the Lutheran's own. But he still lacked the ambition and age to take it to the next level. To the possessed, which is what Threadbare the Lutheran was when it came to Billy and Dampier after he'd first seen them on the Great Salt Flats some eighteen years before. It was all a game to him but why not track it through time and their lives like a study of chronological fear because he was more than a destroyer of man. Threadbare was something that'd grown up from the ground like a mountain. He'd been pushed to the surface by evil and his vision was pure when it came to its practice.

"That's all over Dampier. Those days are done. The man's a memory," he heard Billy say.

"There wasn't any man in him Billy. He never really cared about the price on our heads, he just liked the hunt. He waited too long for us. The really bad ones are always patient you know."

"What do you know about the really bad ones Dampier Mox?"

"I know we've seen the worst. The worst doesn't need a reason Billy."

"Guess not," she replied.

Threadbare moved away because it wasn't a good time to strike. He walked north for six hours before he saw the Percheron lying down on its side in the heat. When the horse heard footsteps it came up on its back legs then threw itself up from the front. As a replacement the Lutheran had taken a middle aged Morgan from the streets of the Soo but the big draft refused to die, snapping at the younger horse whenever it got too close. The Morgan was standing off by itself watching the Lutheran approach. He clapped his hands and it came.

"*Vamos,*" he said.

He grabbed the lead rope of the Morgan and got in the saddle of the Percheron. The larger animal hung its enormous back hoof until the Morgan came within range and then it kicked, the smaller horse falling over on its side and aggravating the Lutheran.

"Stop," he said.

The Percheron turned its head as far as its muscled neck would allow to glance at the Lutheran. Everything in its eyes was indomitable jealousy and pride. He cut the smaller horse loose and rode southeast till night fell.

46

Torq got four of the posse of seven locked into a battle of attrition in some rocks along the Rio Grande and he wouldn't let them out. He sent three of the men north to chase a lone Comanche by stealing a series of horses during the first two days and constantly cutting back in the dust so they'd think it was him. Their leader had little doubt.

"Hamblin, Jimenez and Foretok. I think that's the boy there. That print's deep enough. Follow it till you come up on him and don't pass a soul without askin if they've seen him. Kill him if you get a chance. We ain't takin the little bastard back if he ain't dead."

Torq listened to the Captain's orders from inside the slew of boulders. As they spoke he took off his boots and began to climb over and down until he found what he was looking for.

The rattles came to life twenty feet from the den, hundreds of the creatures spread over one another like cake batter between two small shears of rocks that'd fallen to make the letter A. Their undersides were painted with a hieroglyphic of a hunter throwing his lance at an animal whose fangs touched the ground. The beast in the painting had a toppled man in his mouth.

After two days they couldn't flush him out. The others never returned as Torq watched them stumble over the slick surfaces refusing to remove their boots. They shot up their ammunition at the idea of his presence until the Captain made them stop.

Each man was down to twenty rounds when Torq attacked on the third night, the Captain being bold enough to put his camp in the center of the row of boulders and light a fire after nothing but quick stops while in pursuit. Torq had worn them down and their edge was dulling.

"Gentlemen, the boy is toying with us. He's a game player and a smart ass and I hate this joke of his."

Torq heard every word, giving some respect to the Captain for trying to draw him out, though he'd ultimately have to kill him.

When he smelled the cigarette of the perimeter guard Torq decided he would have to go first. He was lying behind him clinging to the backside of a rock and when he saw the watchman was completely off guard he let go and slid to the ground with a thud. The guard jumped up and fired a round into the darkness, the shot and the calls of the other men masking the sound of rattles.

The snakes were angry when Torq untied the bag, the boy stirring them into a frenzy before running away. The guard heard their warning but had gone too far, grabbing at the sides of the slick boulder but not being able to get a hold with his toe. He plunged down on top of them and was bitten several times before escaping. The man couldn't find his way out of the maze of boulders so he just stopped and panicked as the venom took hold. Torq listened to him cry for help but the others thought it was a trap. They didn't come in till sunup and by that time he was cold.

The remaining three stayed together after they saw the fate of the guard. Their reactions became confused and Torq worked them, alternating between throwing live rattlesnakes and broken chaparral until the men couldn't tell the difference.

He let them sit half the day before he finished it, sending in shots when they took bites of jerky or tried to make water. They had to second guess every move and it wore them down to a singular nerve. Torq's plan had worked perfectly.

Just before noon the Captain exposed himself, taking a hazardous walk across a wide corridor between sets of boulders, the passage wide enough for a horse and long enough for several men to be shot down. He held both hands up knowing Torq was watching and he spoke without thinking.

"Boy! You know this part of the border better than us! But we ain't gonna leave till there's one body or three! Come on, let's end this thing!"

He had a coffee cup in his hand and was holding it up in the air, his guns on his belt and his mouth full of a called bluff. The Captain was a brave man but he'd become dispirited with the passing hours and was making a foolish mistake thinking Torq's fun was just entertainment. This wasn't a battle between the forces of Texas and Mexico and he couldn't call in reinforcements unless he ran into the open and no man did that with a shooter like Torq Mox.

"That's not smart!" Torq yelled from the boulders, wanting him to do better than that. "You can still get out of here but I guarantee if you start that boy talk I'll kill every last one of ya in the next twenty minutes!"

"Don't you take an insubordinate tone with me! I'll have you know..."

"I'll have you know the dead Sheriff's pistol is right on the side of your head!"

A shadow came over the Captain and he could see Torq standing on top of a boulder, his thick frame blocking out the sun. He looked up into his face but couldn't see anything past his inky outline, the long hair of Torq hanging like a towel around his dense neck, the muzzle of the pistol suspended like a punched ticket to eternity in the hands of judgment.

"Test the water before you jump Captain. Go ahead."

Torq put the firearm back into the holster on his left side. He dropped the hammer down gently with his thumb and then put his hands up and turned sideways so the Captain could get a better look.

"I'm big for my age ain't I?"

The Captain flicked his index finger before he went for his Colt. Torq knew he hadn't faced anybody handy with a gun before.

"Don't flinch Capitan! If you go to pull it, don't flinch!"

Torq let the Captain's first shot whiz past his head. The man was so frightened he brought it up to aim. He was taking the second when Torq knocked the cup from his hand. There was a click, then an explosion but no one heard it hit.

"I surprise myself," said Torq.

The Captain looked over at the cup ten feet away. The sand was wet where the flying coffee streaked as it spun. He watched enamored while the sun dried it and then he turned back around. The boy was still there.

"Go ahead, tell the rest to come out of them rocks!"

"You can deal with me first," said the Captain.

"You've been dealt," replied Torq Mox.

The boy's eyes narrowed as he sat down and slid off the top of the big boulder without taking the gun off the Captain. Something flew overhead and replaced Torq's shadow but neither of the men gave it a look.

"Owl," said Torq.

"What?"

The Captain was looking at the boy and the boy at him. There was a shuffle amongst the rocks. Torq knew the other two were moving cautiously to get a shot. The top of one of their hats came into view over the shoulder of the Captain and Torq saw it. The man's boots skidded and as the pebbles fell to the earth he spoke.

"A little quieter out there soldier! Don't show yourself if you wanna shoot me from the front! Be a coward like your other friend here! Not you Captain," said Torq.

The man had stepped out behind Torq fifteen paces away. He could see the Captain to his front change his disposition as hope cleared his sweaty eyes, a thing unacceptable to the current situation in the mind of Torq Mox.

"Yank that shooter again Army ant." Torq challenged, then smiled.

"There's gonna be another killin boy and it's gonna be you. Your reputation stops right here," replied the Captain.

"Your man's dead." Before Torq even finished the words he brought his heels out from under him and dropped from the eyes of the Captain, the movement so quick that the man behind Torq was holding his stomach, gut shot before he even knew the pistol was bucking.

"Fast, ain't I," said the boy.

Torq was sitting on the ground, the smoke from the weapon rising in front of his face. He'd shot with a rapid turn while he was landing on his buttocks. The Captain thought he'd seen him fire underneath his arm without looking but the illusion had created the accuracy.

He kept the gun on the man behind him until he removed his hands three times from the wound, some utterance about the end of life and forgiveness and why these things happen on his thin lips. Torq unwound his body like a rag doll and came back up, stepping forward to hit the Captain in the forehead with the grip of the Sheriff's pistol. The man was still dumbfounded, the resolve vanquished in his eyes.

"Night night," said Torq.

The gut shot man began to stumble down the path leading into the corridor of rocks. When he was a hundred yards away Torq whistled as loud as he could and the man turned.

"You best die out there! Don't make me come and get you! That's a nasty hole I'll add to!"

Torq watched him go forward for another minute and then he fell, his back rising up before he lost consciousness and began leaving the world. He went out and put another bullet in him after making sure the last of the soldiers wasn't courageous, giving him ample opportunity by standing over the Captain and reading some papers in his pocket. He didn't dare risk a shot and Torq knew they were whipped.

"A boatswain taught me my letters on a paddle wheel coming up from French City! That's why I know I'm supposed to be officially deceased by these orders in the Captain's pocket! You stay in them rocks till I go and make sure your friend is done for! Don't leave now! And don't check on the Captain! I just put him down for a bit! He'll get back up!"

Torq didn't return after taking care of the gut shot soldier. He made a five mile loop thinking the man would emerge when it got dark. The Captain awoke before then and when he did the soldier in the rocks saw him get to his feet and dust himself off.

Instead of addressing him the soldier jumped out on his Captain to hide the shame of not having pursued the young outlaw. He meant to parlay the afternoon into a story of unforgettable drama but should've announced his intentions in the queer light, because when he sprang upon the Captain the man put a bullet between his eyes before knowing it was one of his own. After that the officer just sat down and waited. All were dead around him and he'd just killed his own man.

Torq came through later that night but the Captain had already taken care of himself. He took credit for the kill and rode on, stranger things having happened, the disconcerted best soothed without his help and sometimes they were.

47

Billy had the old woman Adivina come out to the homestead to find water. She arrived on the same day that Dampier left the meeting with the railroader's one hundred and fifty miles northwest of San Antonio, still some four hundred miles from Reckingfort Soo. She expected him to attach himself onto a party of easterners looking for new land or to travel quietly at night with Father Epigo if he came across him. Either way it was dangerous, though she felt he'd be safer with the priest.

"He won't be back for another month Adivina. At least a month."

"You be sure and keep that boy close. Watch that Latham," she replied.

She was an old Blackfoot whose father had drifted southeast into Texas when there was a Spanish military post at Goliad and you could find seed bulls for the amateur corridas grazing around the mission at San Antonio. The woman was known for her ability to find water with a flexible cane that came from the wickiups of her ancestors who lived in the sky but couldn't be seen. They told her where the water was and she did the footwork. Adivina often smelled of drink but had pegged the first well at Reckingfort Soo and also at the homestead of Billy and Dampier. They were in need of another for the spring garden if the rain faltered.

"I'm going to let you do what you need Adivina. I'll be inside," Billy said.

"Stay! And go get the boy. I want both of you here when I find it."

Latham was listening from his seat on a stump behind their house. Adivina was more frightening than fascinating to him and he thought his mother a touch eccentric to use her when it was all just a hoax.

"I hear you listening young Latham! Come out from behind there and let me see you."

Latham sat up when she spoke but wouldn't move until Billy came around.

"Come here Latham," she said.

He went to the corner of the house and looked at Adivina standing there with her cane and deerskin boots, her face so wrinkled that if she was more than a hundred he'd give her another fifty years.

"Just because you can't see my eyes doesn't mean I'm blind Latham Mox. What roars in you young man," she asked.

"What?" Latham responded and then looked at his mother. Billy turned her hand over like she was handing his confusion to the old woman.

"Answer," Billy said.

"Nothing roars in me."

"Ahh, then it all went to the other. I could smell something but it wasn't you I smelled."

"The other is dead. You know that Adivina," Billy said.

"Oh, yes he is, is he? Then it must be something else. Must be my Spanish name though I'm Blackfoot. Maybe I roar," said Adivina.

"Maybe you do," responded Billy.

She stopped talking and began tapping her cane on the ground. Adivina asked Billy to roll her a cigarette and when she lit it the old woman placed the smoke in a notch at the end of her cane and held it up to the sky.

"They take smoke you know. You have to please them before they'll talk."

"Adivina, where'd you go when everybody cleared out of Reckingfort Soo that last time?" Billy asked to break the strangeness of Adivina's actions but it didn't work.

"Onto the plains to talk to my father."

"Your dead father," said Latham.

"Bueno," replied Adivina. "You'll learn yet tenderfoot. You're green but growing."

When the cigarette burned down she said they were satiated but hungry. She struck the ground a few more times and then went in the front door and out the back before she froze by the stump. Billy came around to see what was wrong.

"You have water under your house but I told you that last time," Adivina said. "Didn't I tell you that last time?"

"Yes you did," replied Billy.

"It's still there but it's not connected to the one we had success with so don't count on it."

"We can't put a well inside the house Adivina."

"No we can't," she said.

The old woman poked around the yard for a while and then the day grew hot so she stopped, saying nothing before going over to sit in the shade behind the house after a few words about the harsh winter that was coming. She looked like a shell as she slept leaning against the horizontal planks that'd slowly replaced the sod, her hands rigid on her side.

A slow rain came in the afternoon but neither Billy or Latham woke her, allowing her legs to become soaked where they stuck out from the overhang of roof. They'd seen this type of behavior in the old woman before, Latham telling his mother he once found Adivina completely naked on the open plain. He'd tried to go around her but she called him over and told him to remember the shape of woman. He said he would and went on.

Adivina didn't awaken until midnight. She got to her feet and listened to the message in her head and then went over with the cane, looking up at the full moon before she drove the end of it in a spot about two hundred feet from the house.

"The water's here," she said.

The prairie around her was lit up so she walked onto its carpet already knowing the whites would come and divide it up. Their parceling would bring an imbalance and what made it untamed, the very essence of its wildness would become fenced quadrants and in becoming so would cause the land to limp and then die.

"It could be day. The moon's such that it could be day."

She picked up the scent a mile away from the house but didn't bother to turn back. Adivina could smell the rain that'd fallen in the grass and she thought if she were quiet enough she could hear it grow.

The scent grew stronger when she made a slight westerly turn on the compass in her head. She could then see where the grass had been trampled and the deer was shot, its day old carcass left to rot in the sun.

"You took his ball at night didn't you? He hunts at night like the hyena. I've heard men from the east, the ones that come in on the boats tell about the yip yip of the hyena. Did you know he'd shot or was it a clean kill?"

Adivina stood over what was left of the deer and began poking through it with her finger to find the entry wound.

"Through the heart. Good of him if he was going to hunt you in the dark."

She got away quickly and then slowed again when she found the track, following it in concentric circles until it led around the homestead, coming so close to the front and back door she was surprised Billy hadn't seen it instantly. The footsteps were like a roadmap of all the windows and doors on the house. What had been there knew everything about the dwelling and it knew it well.

"Big, still big," she said.

"Adivina, what are you doing?"

Billy was standing in the front door and had been watching the woman for some time. She had a shawl around her shoulders and a tin cup of water in her hand.

"Leaving. I marked your water. Bring the cane when you come to pay me in the Soo."

"I can pay you now Adivina."

"No, not now. Let the cane draw it up for a few days so you don't have to dig so deep when the boys start."

"Just the boy. Just Latham," said Billy.

"I meant when Dampier returns," replied Adivina.

"Oh, okay."

She left without saying another word. Billy could see her profile on the prairie for the next few minutes. The woman lurched and looked down, raising her head to smell the air like an animal before throwing her hand out to ward something off.

"It's so late. So late and she has so far to go."

Billy spoke into the night air and then turned back to her bed. She leaned against the pillow for a moment and looked at Latham in the corner. Before long Billy was asleep.

48

Adivina saw his camp and walked into the firelight. No one had ever come up on him, the old woman being the first in over half a century. Seeing her the Lutheran rose up slowly in the sawing light of the blaze, the ends of a flame singeing his long white hair. He pinched it out with the tips of his fingers and came fully to his feet. It was just before dawn and they were ten miles west of Reckingfort Soo.

"You're close to the road Threadbare. Stripped of it all except age aren't you? The Lutheran rides, yet cannot defeat tick and tock, the fathers of all time."

The Lutheran answered her in Algonkian, the woman not having heard the language of her people for thirty years. Just as she started to answer back the Percheron made its way into the light, its back covered with the grass it'd been sleeping in. Flat palms of orange flame burned in its eyes and the animal came over next to Adivina before the Lutheran called it away.

"It knows only what you do and that's death," she said.

"*A los otros,*" replied the Lutheran.

"Mmm, always the others dying first and never the Lutheran. But you should be careful, I smelled you from a great distance this time. You're careless. Leaving your kill out."

"I wait for the boy," he said.

"He's there for the taking. In the house."

"That's the truth of it. But I smell the other one..."

"Like I smelled you," she interrupted.

The Lutheran stared at her across the fire, its strength rising and falling with the prairie wind. She'd been a fixture on the plain for as long as the Lutheran could remember. He'd ridden down on her at length several times but had never struck Adivina because he was always amazed at the distances she'd wander from her home. The Apache, Kiowa and Comanche considered her something that'd been altered by the sun and hunger so they let her traipse through their camps though she never stopped. He had no idea why she could speak like the whites but he knew if he killed Adivina the oceans might curl up their shores to see where she'd gone. Adivina was a walking piece of magic forever old and mystical. It was dangerous to tamper with her.

"The Kiowa think you can't die," said the Lutheran.

"Immortal," she said.

The Lutheran didn't understand the word so she said it in her tongue. He shook his head and cracked his knuckles.

"I'm not immortal. I just pick up my feet and let the big winds guide. I'm a mother to nothing."

She looked into his fire one more time and then turned to go. Adivina stopped when the Percheron stepped in front of her. The draft horse looked back at the Lutheran.

"He makes his own decisions. He's ancient like you," he said.

She waited several minutes for the animal to make up its mind. It did, but only after a guttural grunt from the Lutheran caught its attention.

"No one comes across the Lutheran. The Lutheran comes across all." She spoke as she made her way into the darkness. He thought he saw her get off the trail but she stayed on.

She'd heard some of the northern rivers were cresting their banks so a week later Adivina left Reckingfort Soo to have a look. She took nothing with her and didn't expect to come back. Soon after one of her own found her. He was off course and heading southeast like Adivina's father had done. The brave discovered her body trampled by hoof but her scalp was intact. There had been no struggle.

When the brave told the next man he met he was drunk in a whiskey house on the Arkansas River. The man he spoke to had heard of the woman and her age and said it was sad that she'd passed.

Another old Blackfoot who'd been listening spoke up from the corner saying magic had also gone with the water woman. He said there had to be a great collision now or all humans would suffer, for whatever took her life would also take the soul of man if it weren't stopped. Everyone agreed that this was true and they went about their drinking in silence.

49

Torq rode his horse to death three days after killing the soldiers because he couldn't find water and wouldn't stop to let the animal rest. He put an X on its forehead with a piece of chalk from one of the soldier's saddlebags and dropped it in the sand with one shot.

He considered smoking the meat but he wanted more to eat than horse. Torq didn't fear another posse but he knew the land could do things to your head so he began to look for tracks and found a set, one leading to a cabin on the South Llano.

The river was dry except for a trickle so he dug down beneath the surface and put his lips in the mud. When he came up his face was camouflaged with the mire and he looked like a castoff from the creation, something left to germinate in a wet place until it took some random shape. The shape of Torq Mox.

"You go up a ways and there's big pools," a voice said. "You've come a good piece I guess?"

"Yes I have," answered Torq.

He didn't look up but continued to watch the mud and water drip from the bangs covering his face. Torq began to wipe his hands down his pants, making sure that his elbows touched the iron of his guns.

"You'll need to not do that," the voice said.

"I do what I please. When and where."

Two clicks at once and the smell of baking bread in the air. Torq could feel the heaviness so he parted the mop of his hair and looked at his aggressor. The man saw his face and nodded.

"The baby killer Torq Mox. There's reward out on you west of San Anton. I outta just fire and collect it but I'd rather see the Rangers chase you up to the big waters. I got plenty of gold myself."

"I may just take it and move on," said Torq.

"I may invite you in for supper," the man responded.

"What do you spend your days doing?"

"Being rich Torq Mox. Being awful rich. All by my lonesome," he said.

He wouldn't give his name after Torq gave him reason to take the guns off him, holding up his hands and saying he'd enjoy a good feed if it were being offered. He thought it best to kill him later when he was comfortable with a little liquor in his veins though he wouldn't be getting that way.

Torq had met his equal, and his equal was three times his age and had lived to remember. The man's every step was singularly prepared for anything and even Torq was somewhat astounded.

"Come in and have a seat. I just finished the house here. The roof still drops dirt in the food but they ain't much I can do about that. Dirt's everywhere and food ain't."

Torq followed him inside and sat at his table. He looked him over but there was nothing to tell. The short build of the man could've been any preacher or dry goods salesman. When he put his guns on top of a bookshelf in the small one room cabin Torq spoke first.

"You're awful trustworthy there goldsmith."

"If I wanted you dead I would've done it yesterday when you were picking across the flats," he replied.

Torq was surprised. "You seen me coming up."

"I've robbed stagecoaches that far away without even firing a shot. You got my tracks and I got yours."

"How'd you do that? Rob the stages?"

"Write a really intimidating letter and make sure it gets to the right people," the man replied.

"That's goddamned crazy," said Torq.

"It's the same as a gunfight only from a distance. Remember, it's always easier to take a kickback from somebody that can afford it rather than a bullet from somebody that can't."

Torq's impetuous youth made him draw on the man for no other reason than he was giving advice. The man heard him think about it and when he did he produced a small single shot pistol from out of the air and had it on Torq before the boy could set the hammer back.

"Don't ever draw with something in front of you. The table would've got you killed. And don't play games. I can't count how many eager Tom's I've put in holes."

"Yessir," said Torq.

"Now strip them guns off since I can't trust you and put 'em outside the door there."

Torq did as he was told, pouting like a child with heavy shoulders. When he came back the table was set with a fresh loaf of bread and butter. Fried white meat sat at his side.

"Where's your stock?"

"Eat," the man said.

They ate in silence for the first five minutes, the man eyeballing Torq like a wayward son. He watched the young killer eat some of his long hair with every other bite. Torq's enormous hands ground into the bread and he wouldn't pick up the fork, spearing each bite or pinching it like a crab before overstuffing his mouth. The filth from his fingers stained his food but he ate on.

"And what of love in a life like yours Torq Mox?"

"If you mean to turn me in or write some fancy story for a paper I'll find a way to kill you. I done that," Torq replied.

"What does somebody like you love? That's my only question."

"You mean whores and such?"

"Can you love a whore?" Torq raised his eyes at the man's inquiry and was returned the same glare, the kind where the eyelids jump and push the sockets into a scowl.

"I reckon I love what's between their legs like any other man," he replied.

"That's ignorance. You're ignorant. The best killing I done was when my wife was alive. Then it was more like a profession than any other time. I could do it more smoothly and with less hate and that always made me faster than a fella that meant to do me in," the man said.

"I ain't equipped to answer such."

"You love the killing too much and you don't love nothing else and that's gonna put you on a goddamned slab in front of a morgue."

"There ain't enough hours in the day for what I can shoot off the prairie. Man or animal, it don't make a damn to me."

"So you know yourself pretty well?" The man asked and then got to his feet to slice a tomato for the boy.

"I can hold my own," replied Torq.

"Boy let me tell you something and then I'm gonna ask you to leave cause I don't want your smell in my walls. I'll send you off with a full stomach, then the advice stops because there's fifty of you for every good man."

"You ain't saying nothing I ain't heard before," said Torq.

"Your violence needs a valve on it boy. Men that go around with a boil like you and no valve to cut it on and off meet matches cause they don't love anything. Now you love the killing because you know no other killer besides yourself. But I tell you the meanest son of a bitch on the face of God's earth ain't gonna ride long if he goes around hot for the next shot. And man's laws don't matter. They ain't gonna get you if you don't want 'em to. But what you got to worry about is the monster that'll run up on you one of these days, one that looks at killing like he looks at a woman. He'll be smitten by it and that's the ugliest kind of violence, the natural kind you see. Do you see?"

"No, not really," Torq said.

"Well, you've been told anyway. Find something to love besides yourself and what it does, which is punish. You just do the killing, but you don't love it like the man you're gonna meet does. He'll understand it and his story will go on and on."

"You don't make no sense at all," said Torq.

"Your days are numbered if you don't respond to what I've said. And it ain't got to be to me."

Torq got up from the table by pushing it away from his body. All of the food fell into the floor but the man didn't move from his work on the tomato. It lay in thick slices and he was reaching for the salt when Torq strapped on his guns and made his way up the riverbed.

He came to one of the big pools the man had mentioned. The trees were as thick around it as if he were in a dark room. Torq drank his fill and then tried to light a broken cigar with a flint but couldn't.

There was an exposed root to his right a man's body could fit under. Torq stared at it until the light left, the sun painting the riverbed, bank and foliage before it made its western dive, all things flowing into the late evening like water falling into a subterranean cavern. The silvers went, and then the pinks. With darkness he went and lay beneath the root and sleep came.

When Torq stood it was early morning of the next day. There was a goat on the bank chewing at some grass behind him and his hunger had risen but he wouldn't consider going back because if he made the same mistakes as the day before he'd be dead. Torq knew the man could get the drop on him. But there was a horse to take and that heightened his interest.

He got up on the bank of the Llano and ran to the back of the man's cabin without a weapon drawn. He meant to see if he was there and if he was Torq would make an offer. If not, he'd return after dark and steal the best mount he had.

"Old man!"

There was no response and no movement from inside. He could see two riders out on the flat some miles distant churning up dust in small clouds. There were several wagons behind them and they were moving northwest at a slow pace, the riders running ahead and then coming back, surging to leave but then staying. Torq saw what he thought was the man in the cabin ride out and begin speaking with the two that ranged ahead but he wasn't sure.

"You in there!" One more time without a retort.

Torq walked around to the front door, turning his head to look at the three men talking before he was stopped brusquely, broadsiding a Palomino with a long blonde mane. A worn Cavalry saddle sat on its back, the trade brand of the Texas militia on its left hip. There was something sticking out between the saddle and the blanket so he reached up and pulled it loose. It was a note from the man in the cabin.

"Go to where you come from," it said.

Torq unhitched the horse and got in the saddle. When he turned up the South Llano he still had hours of daylight left. After a few miles he made a northwesterly turn as the man from the cabin left the company of Dampier and Father Epigo on a rise behind him. Torq had missed his father by five minutes and there was nothing to be said of it.

50

Billy made the trip into Reckingfort Soo just before sunrise, rousting the boy awake and telling him that his breakfast was on the table. The prairie had lulled Latham into inactivity, Billy becoming too complicated in her thoughts to realize he needed something to do besides roam.

"Where are you going?"

"I'm going into the Soo to pay Adivina for the work and I want you digging by seven. Do you understand me?"

Billy stood over his bed while patting the satchel on her shoulder to make sure all her necessities were there. The coals had been stirred in the fire. Some splinters of hog wood sat on top of them and they were beginning to catch.

"Is it cold," Latham asked.

"Getting colder every night. Your daddy needs to hurry and get home before the first freeze hits."

Billy blew smoke into the air and went to their double bed where she pulled on a pair of Dampier's pants, rolling up the cuffs at the bottom beneath her skirt.

"You straddling today?" The boy was on his elbows watching his mother and smiling.

"I ain't got time for hitching up. Is that Western still on the mare?"

"Yessum," replied the boy.

"Well Latham it shouldn't be! How'd you like to stay saddled all damn night and then jumped on?"

"I wouldn't."

"Then don't do it to the horses!"

"Yessum."

Billy walked out looking back at the plate of warmed over eggs steaming on the table in the growing firelight. When the door shut the boy got to his feet and put on his shirt and pants, going over to the front window to watch his mother ride away. Billy expected to see his face. When she did she waved and galloped east.

She noticed the crows diving to the ground just after eight o'clock that morning. Their wings were spread and they were riding the wind, the bird's lithe bodies ignoring the very law of gravity holding them in check. When she went to see what they were diving on she put her pistol on her leg and held it tight.

"I'll be goddamned."

The man had been pulled over a blaze burned out three days and the scavengers had left so the crows were making a game of the remains. Billy could tell he was Comanche by a string of broken beads he'd worn around his neck, the reds and turquoise evident on the ground where he'd died. His genitals had been removed and stuffed in his mouth, the hands tied behind his back, everything on the fire down to bone. The skull was spared and the expression of surprise was still readable.

"I hope the tribes ain't up against themselves," she said.

There was a rub in the grass a few feet from the scene. Something enormous had slept in the spot. She didn't realize how big until her mare walked in the middle of it and was dwarfed. The horse became uneasy with the sights and smells and trotted away. When it turned back to make sure Billy was still there she went and grabbed its ears.

"What?"

The animal nudged her and was frightened, its shoulders trembling. She could hear its heart beating and then she put her finger in her ear. It was her own.

"He needs a grave but we ain't fooling with it. Maybe his people will see him. I don't know who to tell."

Billy looked at the horse for an answer but the animal turned and began leaving her. She chased it up the road and as she did Billy ran through the flat rub and stepped clean of the scene.

51

The place where Adivina lived wasn't locked so she went inside. Nobody answered, the only sound a few voices from the afternoon streets of Reckingfort Soo. There was a greeting, a curse and somebody said thank you.

Billy sat down on the only piece of furniture in the dwelling, the chair creaking under her weight. Light came in interruptive bursts as people walked by outside. The rays looked like they were being unloaded in individual streaks through the cracks in the wall and the room was warm.

There was a single pot in the corner so she stood and picked it up. It was blacked on the bottom but the ash was old. Whatever had been eaten had long since been scraped from the rough surface.

"This ain't right," she said.

Billy asked around but nobody had seen her. She went to the man Hoskins and bought a pint of his liquor and came back to the house to sit down again, smoldering from the looks the man had given her after she'd paid his price.

"Six little ones, a wife beat half to death in the corner and he's getting a rise out of me being there. He should be castrated, the bastard. Sons of bitches the lot of 'em!"

Billy drank the pint and then got her blanket off her horse before going back in. She listened to the mare walk behind the hovel and lie down as the booze swarmed her brain. She was trying to ignore the feeling inside her, what had come back and through and left its calling card. But the corn liquor alleviated all understanding, protecting her as she slumbered, and how brief that time would be.

52

The Lutheran left the Percheron on the plains and walked the streets of Reckingfort Soo after hours. Hoskins was snoring and he could hear him inside his home and smell the cooking of the alcohol and the hungry whimpers of his children. One of them was awake and had come outside to stare up at the moon like an expectant father. He was making water in the dust by its light, that inglorious crater dented circle touchable where it hung in the sky.

In the little boy shapes he drew with his own liquid stepped the Lutheran. The boy's stream fell on his boot but the Lutheran didn't look down, beads of night sweat forming on the filthy forehead of the child and then Threadbare was gone. In the going the child called out like the monster should be a friend and then something in his malnourished brain said don't. He thought it was God so he obeyed.

The boy went inside to wake his mother but she wouldn't rise. There was some mumble from her lips about nightmares and the child said he was fully awake and she said you're bad like your father. He ran back out into the street, the front and then the back but there was no man. How lucky was the child. So many had gone before him and hadn't walked away.

Threadbare knew the house of Adivina so he went and pushed on its door but it wouldn't open, the man closing his hand around a worthless latch before turning it to splinters.

"Anybody home," he whispered.

Billy didn't hear the noise, sleeping on in that doubtful sleep of drunkards and men on the run, not knowing what she might face if she awoke so she settled on the flexibility of her dreams.

He went and stood above her, touching down on her back until she coughed and he let up. The smell of booze was strong in the room but not as strong as the Lutheran's grip, the man flipping Billy over and wrapping his hands around her throat to give a sobering squeeze. She opened her eyes and although it was dark there was enough stench coming from the mouth of Threadbare that she knew he'd returned. But still nothing she thought. Only the worst of nightmares.

"You shouldn't leave the boy alone. He can't fend," said the Lutheran.

"Fend," said Billy in the talk of sleep. Then he was gone.

Billy opened her eyes with the light of morning pounding her temples from the other side of the hovel. She could see the snotty nose of the mare and smell its scent but she couldn't move. The top of her skull felt like it'd been grated and she looked around on the floor to see if the devil had unleashed little demons to do the work. Nothing was there.

The door was standing open and there were people talking in the street and they said the liquor merchant Hoskins had killed himself.

"One of his own found him without a mark. Just dead, like angels come or somethin," a woman said.

"That boy of his told his mama who done it but that young'un is crazy. I think he gets into the still. I really think he does," another remarked.

Billy walked out in the street and into the conversation. The two rough looking females turned to regard her, both lacking the formalities that came with manners, each of their instincts survival and birth and that was it.

"Billy, Billy Mox," one said.

"What of the man Hoskins," Billy asked.

"You heard us."

"Yes Tilly, I heard you," she replied.

Both of the women looked at Billy but she turned away to find the mare. The woman Tilly came around to the back of Adivina's house and tapped Billy on the shoulder, pointing at her throat and keeping her on the ground with one hand.

"That neck of yours is a damndable mess. You've bruises all the way around it. If Dampier takes the hand to you onct he'll do it for the rest of his life."

Billy felt the tender spots on her throat. She said something about Dampier returning from near San Antonio but the woman wasn't listening. She'd turned her back and called the other over to expound on the marks.

"I put a knife in mine the first time he backhanded me. Did it to the second one too," she said. "They ain't kilt though."

"Dampier's not here," reiterated Billy.

"You'll do better with one man," said Tilly. "No woman needs more than one climbin on her like a goddamn chigger."

The other woman added to the comment but Billy ignored her. She bid them a good day and left Reckingfort Soo.

53

While his mother was in the Soo Latham rounded out the spot marked by Adivina and then hacked at the beginning of the well for the rest of the day without stopping to eat. She'd forgotten the cane so he pulled it up and slung it into the grass where it landed and quickly left his mind.

"A water cane, Jesus. What's next?"

When evening came he knew Billy wouldn't be returning. Latham took a pouch of tobacco from a drawer and rolled a short cigarette, taking out a penny book of sketches bought from a European attached to a cow outfit passing through earlier that month. They were drawings of French prostitutes at their work in the bordellos of Paris and the man said he'd made them while they were in the act although Latham didn't believe him.

"There ain't no such thing," Latham had said.

"See for yourself," replied the cowboy.

He lit a candle from the cook stove and went outside, leaving the door open behind him. Latham took a small table to put the candle on, turning his head like a distinguished gentleman to light the cigarette without hands before flipping through the folded sketches in his pocket. He brought a chair out after he saw the third. From the back he was any young man going about his studies. From the front, any young man.

She was lying on a dirty mattress and her hair was the color of the pencil that'd drawn it but her skin was not. The artist had used a vanilla with an odd color blue that made her pulse on the half page like a vein, a monument to everything bursting in Latham down to the very corpuscles of his blood.

"Lordy," he said.

Her suitor was standing next to her and she was looking up at him, his hands on the fly of his pants, the man's eyes averted from some activity going on behind him to look down on the woman's naked flesh. Latham wondered if the artist was speaking to the man, telling him to take the gun from around his waist.

"A pistolero. They're probably in Illinois or something. That's close to Paris I reckon."

There was another drawing of the same scene but the woman was on her stomach laughing. The pistolero was prostrate in the corner behind her grasping at his groin. The artist had put his own leg in the picture and had also added a vase of flowers so colorful it distracted from the nastiness of the sketch and made it easier to look at. He had written his name on the upper left hand side of the page and if Latham could've read his message he would've seen that the series was called "the syph," having little effect on the inexperienced while serving as a warning for the reckless.

The night caught Latham outside with the door still open and his chair leaned back against the house. His sketches were being held down with the candleholder but when it blew out and over they scattered across the prairie, rising high and light on a wind toward Reckingfort Soo.

Latham was tired from digging and never knew they were gone, the wad of gentle leaflets getting up some fifty feet before finally separating and going on their own individual paths.

The picture of the lady with the pencil colored hair outlined in blue, her cursed lover somewhere south on another rip of breeze came back to earth and sat on the road that wound into the Soo. The sketch caught on a reed of munion weed and spun, the night wind blowing her hair where it sat still on the paper. If she would've been living, she would've been pleased. For a short time she was more than her body, she was a photographic tumbleweed with no boundaries, no disease and no mortality. Then she ran into the Lutheran.

Threadbare saw the sketch after its long journey in the night air. He'd ridden the Percheron to exhaustion on his way back from Reckingfort Soo and the animal was breathing heavily beside him.

When he picked it up he turned into the partial light of day and moon to look but nothing stirred him. He noticed the length of his naked arm more than the woman, bringing his fingers down to his holster and then back up again, the front of his shoulder twitching with a spasm of muscle, the hand much quicker than anybody a third of his years.

"Nothing left but a picture," he said.

The Lutheran folded her and put the sketch in the pocket of his vest but the Percheron hadn't gained his wind so he drew it back out. She looked at the Lutheran and the Lutheran at her. He wondered what she was born for and asked in her language but there was no answer.

Finally the horse nudged him with its nose and he had to step forward, turning back to hold the woman up to the Percheron's face but the horse didn't care. There was no affection or appreciation in its look, the same in the countenance of the Lutheran.

When he tore the sketch into pieces and sent the woman back onto the plain day had come, neither the Lutheran or the Percheron knowing anything beyond their own fall, a thing likely not given by any creature they knew. Walking away with the reigns in his hand he watched the woman scatter and continue her journey, pleased he could punish the remembered as well! as the living.

54

Billy couldn't find Latham when she arrived back at the house. She leapt from the saddle and ran to where the new well was, some five foot taken out in a perfect circle but no work having been done that morning.

"Latham! Latham Mox!"

No reply. She kicks around in the grass, each lick of her foot knocking down some tendril growing from the earth since the exit of the waters. Grass she thinks, miles of it and my child upon it like a piece of thread in a vast carpet.

"If he's been taken I'm done with this damned settler's life. I'll mix in somewhere, somewhere where he won't come back, and then back again," she says.

Billy finds the water cane of Adivina and her eyes are tired but she reads the etchings on its side, some mark for each time the stick brought forth God's secrets and they're many, too many Billy thinks. She drives it in the ground with the palm of her hand and sits to smoke where a fence was being built and she laughs at not having completed the project.

"Mama?"

Latham rides up behind her silent like his father. Billy rises and walks over to hug one of his mounted legs with a tear on her cheek. He ignores it like he doesn't need it and acts tougher than he is. She returns to her seat adding no words to her fear.

"Are we going to start back on this fence? Is that why you're out here?"

"No, no reason. I'm just sitting. Too young for the years that've passed. Too young," replies Billy.

The boy doesn't understand but as he looks he notices her throat and the bruises and he guesses she's been with another because his daddy's told him not to trust the feminine wile but he loves his mother. As they frown at one another there's a rumble in the air. Storm clouds are gathering in the distance as Latham starts to ask why she's crying but doesn't.

"Rain's coming," he says.

"It comes, it goes," Billy answers from the ground.

"Mmm hmm," he replies.

"Adivina wasn't in."

"She wanders a whole lot. The pastor says she'll go a season and not come back," Latham added.

"She ain't coming back from this last one," Billy said.

"Moved?"

"You could say that Latham."

Billy's legs fall asleep as the clouds block the sun and a light drizzle begins to fall from a smattering of dark. Latham doesn't move but watches as his mother's hair catches droplets of water which run down her face and hands like they're circulating with her blood. She sits until she's soaked and it goes through her shirt but the two remain fixed and it becomes strange like they've given up their lives and are waiting to be plucked from the prairie but nothing comes to do it just then.

They only rouse when the sky shoots its first bolt of lightning and then they move quick, having seen it pick one cow out of a hundred, that one dropping and smoking from its mouth and eyes as others looked on and in their bovine stupidity never wondered why it wasn't them, sluggishly pleased they hadn't been touching the dead animal.

When mother and child are safely inside nothing is said about the little boy mess of the house or the crumpled covers of the unmade bed. They sit at the table and Billy looks over glad the fire is burning.

"We should reach up and move the damp I reckon," said Latham.

"It's too hot in the chimney, just let it go," replies Billy.

They watch the droplets begin to cascade into the open flue and sizzle in the fire. Billy looks at Latham like she's got something to say and then she withdraws, holding her arm out to ask if he'll sit in his mother's lap but he won't.

"What mama? What is it?"

"Latham, I..."

Billy stops and is right on the edge of telling him the history of herself as mother and Dampier as father but she won't jump in. He's looking at her with his heavy brow and hair that's leaning toward black like the heart of his brother. She sees in his eyes the innocence that the killer Torq missed, though Billy knows they have the same hands and structure and that the child taken from her was more vicious but still the child. Each boy turns in her womb poetically like the day before their births and she'll never see differently.

"What do you know mama?"

"Don't push!"

"What do you know mama?"

There's a long pause as it builds and it builds tall and thick.

"I'll tell then. Okay," she says.

When the story comes it takes an hour in one continuous stream and it is both ugly and intriguing, like finding a hole in a roof where a drip comes from and stopping its progress. Though she wouldn't give Latham all the days she gave him most, her time in the territory of Oregon and how the cough took her people and what wandering can sometimes get you. When she met his father and how the shooting brought the Lutheran's bloodlust, its results dropping people in their path that the devil himself had rejected.

"There was this place called Mims Nickel you see. A fort I guess, a prison, no, a place where the ire of the meanest got to be heard, acted out. Do you understand? We're no more guilty than the next."

The boy wrinkled his forehead when the lines got crossed and Billy stopped, answering questions like if her Dampier was still a killer what had led him away from God. Billy responded by saying he wasn't but he was, and that in her haste much of the horribleness had come but Latham wouldn't believe her. She thought she'd left out the worst parts but Billy was unsure.

"And then we came here son. We were the first and that's something to be proud of."

Latham was mulling it over like there wasn't enough time to get the answers and then he brought it down to one. He stood up like the man he was becoming and went over to stand in front of the fireplace till his clothes began to smoke and when they did he spoke.

"This Threadbare. Threadbare the Lutheran. I know of him."

"He took your brother off," said Billy. "He took him off and now he's come back."

"He's passing through?"

"Son, he never passes through. He wants to end this thing. I think he's toyed with us enough."

"And you and daddy ran? You ran from what he done?"

"We've paid ten times for what we've done Latham. Some days a hundred."

"It don't make it right though does it?" Latham was vexed and just needed to hear it, the challenge to everything he knew was right. The boy had already completed most of the story but the details had always eluded him.

"No it don't Latham. It sure as hell don't."

"But he ain't got no right to keep on you and daddy."

"I guess not," Billy responded.

"Did you think he came after me mama?"

"I thought..."

The galloping was heavy like anvil shots and they could hear it when the rider was minutes away. Billy got to her feet and slid the bolt shut on the front door and then went around to the windows. Latham tried to help but was sat back down and told to be quiet by his mother.

With the rider came the heavy rain and before they knew it they were in the eye of the storm, the sheets of water pounding on the roof in such a thunderous tumult that Latham moved over to be by his mother, shadowing her small body and holding her thin wrists.

Slow droplets of water began leaking on the table but they made no plans to mend it, sitting in near darkness with no sound until the eiderdown heaviness of a clothesline blanket slapped to the muddy ground outside.

"Nothing to it Latham, just the weight of the water brought it down. It must've been a cowpoke or a brave passing," Billy said.

"Must've mama. I barely heard it."

They waited for an hour but the rain didn't slacken. Billy was rewriting her life in her head and Latham was watching, seeing every stop and turn the woman had made, every decision that brought about this and that, one of them the very act giving him life. Then suddenly there was no more rain.

"I done the best I know how Latham."

"I know you did mama."

Latham's voice lifted above a whisper and when it did the blast from the horse's nostrils sounded through a crack in the door, the snort followed by a kick and a shot, the bolt left to dangle without a slide, the bottom half of the door flying upwards into the room.

"In the back of the house Latham!"

They jumped behind the bed, neither thinking to draw a weapon or sprint through the rear of the house. Beneath the bed they saw one boot and then another drop from the horse. Billy had her mouth on Latham's ear and she was panting.

"So quiet Latham. Be so very quiet."

The rider examined his work and then the feet were gone, the horse remaining still for a moment before being pulled away. All lay tomb quiet, the breath of mother and child suspended in the air like a perfect knot.

"You need salvation."

The voice was behind them, through the wall. It was deep and lethargic, like the very chest it came from was filled with the fluid of hate. It destroyed a small piece and was gone. All that was left was the sound of the leak and the horse's departure, less heavy in leaving as their ears came back to the crackling fire.

55

Mother and son waiting, staying close to the house, so close that when thirty of their stock are rustled along with three ponies they lie awake and listen to them stampede, the sound coming through a busted door splintered some seven days past. The steers and the horses are run through their yard and the rustlers call out to Billy saying they'll trade the herd for a piece of her body but she pays them no mind.

"To hell with them," says the boy. "They're all criminal whites moving west and they can't get their own goddamned stock. Why have they got to say such?"

"Language Latham!"

"Damn them each and every one to hell!"

Billy gives the command then subdues herself without correcting him again, paying no more attention from her place on the bed. Latham fumes and perches his musket on a window frame to touch off a shot that goes into the darkness where there's a scream and then a fall.

The rustler receiving the lucky ball gets on his feet and begins running down his mount, firing back a bullet that wallops against the side of the house. Latham wants to return it but is stopped by his mother.

"Don't invite that Latham! Let 'em have what they want! They'll get their share directly." Billy is adamant and bleary eyed with the seriousness of a lost child. The boy backs off and listens to his mother but he isn't through.

"It's been a week mama. He's gone on."

"Are we still living Latham?"

"We are," says the boy.

"Then you know he ain't gone," she replies.

The rustlers run the animals for ten miles and then slow at the Mox's watering hole where the one that's shot says he can't go anymore. All three rustlers are what Latham said they were, men broken off from eastern settlers. Transient vagabonds who drank too much or raped or committed atrocities on the children of the Choctaw. All had been tossed from their caravans and had to survive on their own, the plains as unfamiliar to them as the western peaks they'd never get to see.

The one with the ball in his chest is named Vestry Dor and he was once the son of a prominent colonel from Virginia but he is no more. His chances in this life have been numerous but he's chosen to pursue the violent and the violent he has found.

"You sons of bitches leave me and I'll give you up to the first lawman I see!"

Vestry Dor looks at his two acquaintances who are watching the animals water but they won't look back at him. Each man slowly moves off with short wings of cattle and before Vestry Dor knows it he's alone by the rainwater pond, his chest heaving and leaking, the ball positioned to kill him.

"Just pull it out! Come pull the goddamned ball out and I'll heal up! Don't leave me here! Minzo! Top! Help me!"

They're out of earshot but he screams in pain for some time, his shirt becoming soaked with blood. The men Minzo and Top are gone with the rustled stock, each knowing they'll ride the plain that night because they didn't draw near the injured man who would've killed them and taken the prize for himself, for there is no camaraderie between the insulted or the insulter and any man on that raw frontier who places himself in harm's way will receive what he asks for. And that includes your brothers who've left you Vestry Dor. Yet the same rules don't apply for the one that's coming to help.

"I can get that out," the voice says.

"I bet you can," says Dor.

He thinks Minzo has circled back when he hears the man speak. Instead of turning he looks at the reflection of the half moon on the water and reaches for a smoke but has none.

"You got any tobacco on ye? Bleedin makes a man want a fried steak and a big ol' smoke."

The hand reaches over the shoulder of Vestry Dor and lays a rolled cigarette in his palm. He doesn't think to ask why the man isn't discussing the cattle or the direction they should go and when they should stop. Dor's beginning to get woozy and the words won't come as he lights the smoke and draws in a long pull.

"Could you go ahead and yank this out? I ain't doin so awful well. Where's Top?"

"No problem," the man behind him says.

"I said where's Top!"

When it finally dawns that he isn't in the company of familiars the man behind him walks around to Vestry Dor's front and straddles his feet, the stench falling from his hunched over shoulders and long stringy hair. The night is chilly so he wears the wrap of a bruin shot by a trapper who wished him a good day. His face is clean but smudged to fight off the wind and all the elements that come for man and animal from the emptiness of the plain. He's been awake watching and riding while gutting the insides of a panoramic and growing Texas with the hooves of so many different horses he can't remember the last one he rode until it claws the ground behind him. He's surprised to have come so far and seen so few.

"Who the hell are you," Vestry Dor asks.

"A traveler," the man responds.

"Can you help a fella out?"

"I've helped many a man in times of need."

The man pulls out a long and curved blade, the tip of it bent from packing his own shot on rocks along the Rio Grande. Without permission he pins Vestry Dor on his back with a boot heel and before he knows it the blade is in his chest flicking the ball in the dirt but Vestry Dor is losing sight of the rancid physician. The cigarette drops down onto his arm and burns him but he doesn't feel its heat.

"Where'd you and them other two pick up that herd? I know them brands," says the longhaired man.

"You ain't gettin none of my take! I don't care if you did save me," replied Dor.

His determination is wasted on his savior because with the removal of the shot an artery is compromised without apology. Vestry Dor wears a bib of his own life's blood but nothing can be done.

"How do you feel?"

"Think I feel," says Dor.

The rider puts his finger in the hole and then curls it to press with his palm, the pressure stopping the bleeding momentarily. He reaches around and picks up the knife and puts it behind the ear of Vestry Dor, coming across the front of his hairline, the back of the blade making a meridian without cutting while he measures his parameters. Vestry Dor watches him with what eyes he has left before the man's face comes into the light. Dor looks at him and the man nods.

"Who are you," asks Dor.

"Nobody special. And don't worry, I'll cut your friends out of their fair share too."

There's a scream muffled by the hide of the bruin and then Vestry Dor is no more. The body is thrown feet first into the watering hole where it spins face down and bubbles.

"Goddamn that brother of mine is a horrible shot!"

Torq Mox smacks his lips and turns into the night, wiping the blade clean before returning it to hiding.

"Closer now," he says.

56

Billy concedes they are prisoners in their own house but it has to stop, her best solution to have Latham fix the door. They decide to cut another one from some felled oak dropped somewhere in Appalachia. The wood has sat since they came by their money and land and they were saving it for something special. Latham thinks that occasion has come and though he's no carpenter he jokes with his mother about what he's best at and she smiles.

"Daddy won't care if we use it for the door. It'll probably be a little off since I'm used to sitting and watching cattle. But I'll do the best I can."

"You can do more than that Latham Mox. We raised you right."

"Better than Torq," he replies.

Latham is standing in the doorway and the noon sun is on his back so he looks like an angel to his mother. When he says it she puts her face in her hands and great sobs follow but the boy doesn't go over. He's seen enough of the cloak and dagger between his parents and he knows he can't correct the lies of others so he lets her sit with her falsehoods and she does.

"I didn't mean it like it sounded," he says.

"I know you didn't. Go do what you want. If you don't get the first cut flush then do another. There's enough of it for ten doors."

Latham goes to their small shed and grabs a saw and an axe, its handle cut from a pignut tree. Dampier's branded his name on the lower part and as Latham remembers their day together he recalls a hundred others, each event coming and going and it makes his heart heavy so he sits down.

He can see his mother standing in the door watching him, her weighted cheeks and disappointment clinching to her like it wants to pull her to the ground. He gives a quick wave and all that was angelic about him dies, the clouds staining his cheeks so he looks like his brother Torq.

Billy sees the other boy in his face with the angle of the sun but he's still her Latham so she brings back the grin. And then it all came down like a wanton blizzard of mayhem.

"Mother!"

Latham leaps to his feet and he's pointing and beginning to run but Billy doesn't react. Cords of light fall across her back and then there's a quick snap and she vanishes from the doorway. It shuts and the broken part flies outward and then back down. When he gets to the clothesline next to the house he's tripped with a lash from a bullwhip and then pulled behind the shed screaming and twisting, the assailant of such strength Latham can't bring his head free until it jumps over him and puts him face down so he'll be quiet.

"Goddamn you Latham, shut up. If you don't she's dead."

The voice knows his name and won't let up until Latham straightens his fingers to signal his silence. He's then given a quick look from his stomach backwards, a rapid jerk that puts him eye to eye with his brother, the sockets of Torq the same as his but there's something extra there, something pensive and icy.

"It's me you lil' bastard. If you don't quell that bitching and yelling he'll cut her throat. He ain't leaving till he gets all of us, but I don't need no help killing him so settle down."

"Why're you here?"

"I knew you'd ask a bunch of goddamn questions. It'd do me better to wipe out the whole family but then Dampier wouldn't leave me no inheritance now would he? They ain't no time for that now. We got us a problem."

Torq slid off his brother's back. Latham started to push him but then restrained himself when he took a look at the boy who appeared to be twenty years older, a full neck and shoulders like a bulls growing from the side of his head, so much gristle on his youthful frame he made two of Latham.

"You're puny," said Torq.

"Christ Almighty," replied Latham.

Torq called a challenge to the house but then searched through his experience and decided on another tack. Latham began offering a brief history of the Lutheran that brought the glare of the killer Torq and shut him up before he got started.

"I know Latham. Better than most I know."

There was a softness with the words, Latham lifting his hand to clap his brother on the back. His wrist was caught before it fell.

"Don't," said Torq. "I won't think twice about it boy. I'm not family to you or them."

Latham was nose to nose with the steam and vengeance in Torq's eyes. He could see every atrocity he'd committed and it scared him down through the soles of his shoes and his brother smelled it.

"You stink of fear so stay out of the way."

Torq stepped into the open and pulled his sidearm from its holster. He dropped in five shells while he walked, hoping the Lutheran was watching. When he was fully loaded he goaded the bounty hunter by whistling both the Percheron and his own mount into the yard.

The Percheron got there first, not stifled from what it wanted to do by any command from inside the house. Its enormous head was swinging from side to side as it trenched the length of its body in the dirt with long, even scrapes. Snot was flying from its nose, all of the draft's muscles tense and trembling.

"Charge you son of a bitch," said Torq.

"Kill it now," yelled Latham.

When the Percheron's eyes turned to circular blood and it came up on its back legs Torq did nothing. He stepped forward in its path when the beast was thirty feet away and then he leveled the pistol and fired, the first shot striking the skull of the Percheron between the ears but still it came.

"I've waited for this," said Torq.

The next two shots sent the horse careening beyond the living and then it slowed to a trot and dropped at the feet of Torq, the ground shaking and sending him to balance with one hand. The other horse came over to sniff it and when it did the Percheron bit upwards one last time and then died, its last flash a bloody red sun that shut its eyes forever.

"Straight to the devil's stable. I'll see you there," added Torq.

The Lutheran watched it all with a hand full of Billy's hair and didn't flinch. She held back her emotion without saying a word as she dangled from his cold grip, the man's enormous face pressed against the shutter of a window, peering outside as the Percheron was gunned down by Torq, watching as the boy reloaded his spent shells and then put another one in the back of the animal's head.

"That's done," said Torq.

"That's done," repeated the Lutheran.

"Me and you then! I ain't got no rub with these folks! Just you! You hear me?"

The Lutheran listened to Torq and then looked down at Billy who looked up at him, the end of her finger still scarred where he'd bitten it off all those years ago. It rested on his upper arm and pushed down when he hurt her but he wouldn't release just yet.

Billy saw that his hair was the same ghost white, still long like it could reach for you. There were lines around his face, age adding no hint of humanness in those twisted eyes. She looked down to see if he was wearing what she remembered the first time she saw him but he wasn't.

"Mother. Mother of the twins," he said.

"Do what you've got to Lutheran. The only son of a bitch that can kill you is right outside. He came from me and that's the best I got."

The Lutheran found her words ironic though his mind was coated with a tapestry of vileness letting few original thoughts past its thick plexus of rage. He stood her up and when she buckled again he slung her from the floor onto the bed, her head hitting a post as she flopped onto the planks without moving. There was a bottle of cheap whiskey on the table and he went over in the darkness of the room and pulled the cork from it with his barred teeth and emptied the fiery contents down his long throat, throwing the bottle into the low burning fire, a stab of short flames jumping up and then changing into smoke.

When he stepped through the door and knocked it off the hinges Torq squared himself. They regarded each other's similarities as the Lutheran came into the sunlight twenty paces from the young killer and faced him, the wind from the whiskey and the foul sense that wafts from lower hell impregnating the yard with everything bad in one confined space. Their regard for one another equaled that of two flailed and maddened crocodiles in a thimble full of water. There was going to be no true winner, just the heightening of each man's need for singular carnage after they'd slain so many. The best was going to be improved upon, no one having any idea who'd stop what walked away, nothing having equaled either to this point in time so make your choice. Prior opinions are worn like risk.

"Time to end you Lutheran. Time to end all this."

"The apostle Torq," replied the Lutheran.

"I need you out of the way. Out of mine. Out of the worlds."

"I need you not boy," said the Lutheran.

The old and the young, something having gone wrong since they left the care of others, since they became themselves but neither will agree. There's nothing around them but silence and in that quiet each selects his method, the Lutheran raising his clublike hand to pull at his ear and when he does he returns with a revolver from his back and fires once at Torq. The boy swears he sees the shot leave the barrel and the snap of fire and oil from the muzzle but before he can react he's hit and it burns in the front of his leg and then there's no feeling at all, just a dull ache and the slow motion excitement of the Lutheran thumbing back the trigger to fire again but he stops.

"Boom," he says.

Torq is hopping and moving sideways, sacrificing his draw by his direction. He's confused and hasn't seen anybody this fast though he's heard stories, the memory of the old man on the South Llano coming to mind but his games were less permanent. The boy is asking himself where the pistol came from and he cannot answer as he continues to watch the Lutheran and bounce sideways for a cover he won't get to in time, the bead of the other man's gun on him and that man smiling because he's won.

"These things are not regular, not orthodox," announces the Lutheran.

Torq's surprised at what the man said, like he's telling him to not stand down a gun as if he didn't know. But he can only think of going for the side of the house, the Lutheran following him with the gun up and the trigger back as the animal's of the plain pay no attention to the men, a blue bird crossing into the sky where it sees a bird of prey and comes back to earth.

"Do it! Go on! Don't make no goddamn spectacle outta this!"

Torq is yelling and beating on the leather of his holster as the Lutheran's eyes wait for him to skin it with an odd respect for a fellow killer. Still the boy won't, he's trying to get out of it, the hopping and the fresh new pain in the leg all he can stand as blood begins to fill up his boot and he reaches out for the corner of the house he was born in, the shoulder of the Lutheran slamming into its side at the same moment, twisting to see the mother of young Torq standing by the bed with her own weapon leveled to fire but waiting, expecting and wanting to see the Lutheran's face as she unleashes a cartridge from the shotgun through the open window, the blast filling up the dark house with light and throwing the Lutheran backwards and then down. His chest floods with numbness and his legs won't move though he tries to stand. Breathing heavily he waits and then hears her voice.

"That'll be enough of that," says Billy.

She walks through the door and stands over him knowing what damage she's done. The Lutheran looks into her eyes and while he's looking Torq comes into his vision with his gun pulled. He puts it against the side of the Lutheran's head but Billy stops him.

"No," she says. "Go get your brother."

He can hear Torq Mox dragging his bad leg away without saying a word. When he's gone Billy comes back to his eyes and he grits his teeth as the numbing continues but no words are exchanged. Finally he reaches out and wraps his hand around Billy's ankle. There's an attempt to go for a short knife in his belt but his hand won't grip.

"No return. Enough," Billy says.

She puts the shotgun to his face and shuts his eyes forever. The Lutheran hears it, sees it and feels one last charge from his mind before he's off to where men walk and wonder to feel the heat from volcanoes though they trek beneath the moving penumbra of oblivion's snow.

57

Latham comes from behind the shed and catches his brother before he falls. Billy steps over the Lutheran's body and helps bring Torq inside the house, lifting one of his arms and placing it around her shoulder.

"Slowly child."

Latham pulls back the cover on his parent's bed and they lower him down, his face pale and his eyes spinning in their sockets. The wound in his leg is clean but he's lost blood. They look for a bullet and then dress it while he's passed out.

"It went through. Must've glanced off a bone but it don't look broke," said Billy.

"I ain't done no doctoring myself," responded Latham.

"Me neither. Well, what I had to I guess."

They wait through the night with the brother and the son, each of them dosing at intervals and then popping up to see he's still breathing. Torq's horse circles outside and becomes upset with the dead animal and human in its midst so around dawn Billy asks Latham if he'll drag off the Percheron.

"If I can get it hitched will you come with me to bury it," he asks.

"We ain't going to bury it Latham. I want you to put it in that cleave where the sandwash is. Then burn it. Do you understand?"

"Yes mama. Will you go?"

"I'll go if he's living."

By the time Latham gets the work done Torq's chest is heaving at a steady pace and his pulse is strong. Billy comes outside and tells Latham she's going. They walk beside the horses for an hour until they come to the wash.

"Take the harnesses off our horses and put 'em in with that goddamned animal. Use the lamp oil I brought and set the whole thing on fire. Use all of it. Throw on some brush if you have to."

"But mama, those are expensive and daddy says..."

"I'll take care of your father," she replies.

Billy walks back as Latham does the rest. When she arrives she agonizes over the body of the Lutheran but he'll not rise again. In the late afternoon she can see the deep dark smoke from the fire and she's pleased Latham got it going. There's a fleck of flame on the edge of the horizon and she thinks she sees him circling the wash but Billy's tired.

Latham gets back before nightfall, both of them going in to stand over Torq, his face in a visage of death though he continues to live.

"The man outside is next," Billy says.

"Burn him?"

"Once and for all."

The Lutheran is rigged with ropes and drug out to the pyre by his ankles. By the time they get there the Percheron has been skinned down to the bone but there's enough fire to send the Lutheran to ash. He's rolled on top of the horse in the deep gully and when he lands his arm is thrown over his companion's flank like he's sleeping with the beast as they turn to leave.

"We never mention this Latham. This is for us and your brother."

"Yessum."

When they get back to the house Torq is gone from the bed and his horse from its place in the yard. Billy says nothing, instead she looks into the night, putting her finger behind her and asking Latham to please pull off the bloody sheets and put them in the washtub. He pauses and forms his statement, the boy misunderstanding his sibling as much as his mother.

"Maybe he'll come back."

"Why," asks Billy.

Latham doesn't answer.

58

Four hours later Dampier and Epigo arrive and awaken Billy. They can see Latham sleeping on a cot in the corner but say nothing about the quilt that hangs over the door. Billy gets up and kisses her husband, putting her hand on the shoulder of Father Epigo who's sitting pensively in front of the fire.

"Epigo," says Billy.

"Hello Billy. Sorry to come in so late. We broke off from the caravan and came on."

"That's okay."

Billy makes coffee and asks if they're hungry but they say no. Each of the men smoke but Billy refrains, leaning her head over to sip from a saucer instead of bringing it to her mouth, her eyes meeting the men's as they make comments about the trip and their plans and where this next year will find them.

"Was there somebody coming from out this way Billy? Eastbound? We saw a rider."

Dampier asks and puts his hand on Billy's arm but she doesn't immediately answer. The room is quiet and they can hear Latham breathing. They all look at the boy and Epigo smiles.

"Nobody that's been here," she says.

"Did you all burn today? We saw the fire coming in," adds Dampier.

Billy gets up to refill their cups. When she turns around Latham comes to his feet from a deep sleep and stretches, walking over to tap his father on the shoulder and speak directly into his eyes.

"Some settlers came through on their way west and asked if they could burn a mule that got snakebit. I told 'em where to go and they said thank you. Did you have a good trip?"

"Yes son, it was fine. Was there anybody with a bit mule in our group Epigo?"

"Not that I recall, but my recollections stay muddy Dampier."

"As do mine," added Billy.

The End

Epilogue

November 9th, 1850. California's statehood is two months old and the people are streaming westward as if they'd been released from a pressurized container. All except one.

His purview tells him they'll never build on these ruins of Mims Nickel. As he looks out on them he understands that there's more beneath the early ice glazing the burned wood of the fort. He's uneasy with all the stories he doesn't know because he was off by himself when they brought the convicted here as if solitude did expunge his thoughts.

"We ain't in California," he says.

When he speaks his horse perks up its ears and looks at his face but the man doesn't continue. Amongst the ruins he builds a fire and through the evening he watches it but sleep doesn't come.

During the night another lone figure places its body amongst the rocks and won't come out. The old man by the fire sees it like he sees the shadows and calls to it but there is no response, only the lighting of some ember in the distance that charges something else and is gone.

"Hey! Come to the fire! Come up to the fire! Ain't no need to stay out yonder by your lonesome!"

Placed between the history of the rocks the other is at home, watching men kick out what warms them with frozen boot heels and then move away from what he is and that's all their fears. They see what he casts and although he threatens them, he is no worse than what they themselves create in their own minds. He is the devil they want and the one they order with every sin.

"Well goddamn you then! Stay in them rocks till it all freezes! I ain't stayin around to be kilt!"

He lets the man move off and he can hear the whinny of his horse and smell his filthy body as they cross the plain. He has no animal so he stands in the dying fire and it lights up his face but it is nothing for you to see. The choked blaze stands him out on that tundra as he looks down into creation at what the first man dared to carry. He picks up a log and blows with burned lips on its thick end and it comes to life, procreated like the coming of the universe. When the log burns down he throws it back on the heap, stamps the fire into submission and moves off to the east in the darkness that brought him.

Look back saint, something worse is closing and all the odious expands.

§

Printed in the United States
41679LVS00006B/154